THE
REBEL CAPTAIN'S
ROYALIST BRIDE

Anne Herries

MILLS & BOON

Published in Great Britain 2014
by Mills & Boon, an imprint of Harlequin (UK) Limited,
Eton House, 18-24 Paradise Road, Richmond, Surrey, TW9 1SR

© 2014 Anne Herries

ISBN: 978 0 263 90947 0

Harlequin (UK) Limited's policy is to use papers that are natural, renewable and recyclable products and made from wood grown in sustainable forests. The logging and manufacturing processes conform to the legal environmental regulations of the country of origin.

Printed and bound in Spain
by Blackprint CPI, Barcelona

Anne Herries lives in Cambridgeshire, where she is fond of watching wildlife and spoils the birds and squirrels that are frequent visitors to her garden. Anne loves to write about the beauty of nature, and sometimes puts a little into her books, although they are mostly about love and romance. She writes for her own enjoyment, and to give pleasure to her readers. Anne is a winner of the Romantic Novelists' Association Romance Prize. She invites readers to contact her on her website: www.lindasole.co.uk

Previous novels by the same author:

Prologue

James Colby stood by the grave of the woman he had loved, then bent to place a single delicate flower on the grass, which now covered it. He had come to say his final farewell before riding off to the war and an unknown destiny. Perhaps before too long had passed they would lay him in the earth beside his sweet Jane and the sorrow he had known these past eighteen months or more would be ended.

'Forgive me,' he whispered as a gentle breeze seemed to stir and grief caught his throat. 'You were too young and lovely to die. If a life was forfeit, it should have been mine.'

For a moment the sun came out from behind the clouds and it was as if a kiss grazed his cheek. He seemed to see the face of the girl he'd loved and hear her voice.

'You were not to blame, my dear one,' the voice said close to his ear. 'Forgive me that I was too young and foolish to wed you when you asked.'

James cried out in agony. For she was so close that he could almost touch her, and he wanted to breathe life into those white lips, to bring her back to the world of sun and laughter.

The world was so much less without the innocent, gentle girl he had loved and cherished with all the tenderness of calf-love. Turning away, his heart wrenching because he must leave her there, James began to think of the months and possibly years ahead. The war was certain now that King Charles had set up his standard. He had tried to arrest the five members of the Houses of Parliament and his action had led to outrage and an upsurge of feeling against the tyrant who believed that only he could judge what was best for England.

'What is best for Charles Stuart more like,' Cromwell and Hampden had said when James talked with them about the future. 'If the people of this country are ever to be free from tyranny, we must rise up and fight for our principles.'

James could only agree. He enjoyed his life

as a landowner, a man of peaceful habits who had no wish to argue with his neighbours, but he now understood that for his way of life to continue he must fight. The King had imposed unfair taxes to fund his disputes and laws that were biased against the common man. Although James would have preferred not to take up arms, he knew he had little choice for soon the whole country would be split.

Besides, perhaps some action would ease the ache about his heart and the sense of having failed Jane, though he did not know what he might have done differently.

Donning his hat, which had a wide brim and a curling feather, James walked away from his betrothed's grave. He did not think he would return again. He must put the unhappiness of Jane's death from his mind and begin his life again.

Lost in his thoughts, he did not see the shadow lurking behind a huge oak tree at the edge of the graveyard, nor did he see the expression of hatred on the man's face.

'You killed her, James Colby,' the man said out loud as he watched him walk away. 'You were responsible for her death—and because of that I shall kill you one day soon…'

Chapter One

Babette was in the orchard, pulling ripe plums, when she caught sight of a small party of horsemen riding towards her uncle's house. Calling to her cousin, Angelina, and their servant, Jonas, to follow, she picked up her basket and walked hastily through the orchard to the kitchen gardens of the modest manor house. She'd seen the figures outlined against the ridge of the hill some distance away and was not sure whether the soldiers were Royalist or Parliament men.

'Aunt Minnie,' she cried, 'there is a party of horsemen riding fast towards us. I do not know whether they be Cavaliers or rebels. Where is my uncle?'

'Sir Matthew has gone down to the long

field. They are cutting the wheat today. Had you forgot?'

In her haste to return and warn her family, Babette had completely forgotten that her uncle had decided to set the men to cutting his wheat. Because Sir Matthew Graham had not chosen to fight when King Charles set up his standard, some of his neighbours suspected him of being for Parliament and the Royalists amongst them eyed the family suspiciously when they attended church.

It was everywhere the same in a country torn by civil war. The quarrel betwixt King Charles and his Parliament had blown up suddenly the previous year, seemingly out of nowhere, except that Aunt Minnie's second cousin, Henry Crawford—who was close to his Majesty—said that the trouble had been brewing beneath the surface for a long time. When the King tried to arrest five members of Parliament only to discover the men he considered traitors had been warned and fled, he decided that only a war could bring these unruly men to heel.

'Whatever shall we do?' Babette's aunt asked, looking flustered. She wiped her hands on her apron. 'Should we lock the doors against them or welcome them as friends?'

'It depends who they are and what they want,' Babette said, though in truth she was not sure which side her uncle would choose if forced to take sides. Babette knew her own heart, but for the moment she kept her silence. 'I think Jonas should go to my uncle with all speed and tell him that visitors are on their way.'

Aunt Minnie agreed and Jonas was told to saddle the old grey cob, which was the only horse not already in use in the fields, and ride to alert his master.

'Will they kill us all, Mama?' Angelina asked, looking frightened.

'God have mercy, child! I hope not,' Lady Graham replied, but her face was pale, and she looked at her only daughter anxiously. 'We must lock all the doors, Babette. Maria! Alert the other servants. Close all the doors and windows. We shall not open them until Sir Matthew comes home to tell us what to do.'

Babette hurriedly locked and barred the kitchen door. Three ladies alone in the house, apart from a few female servants, could not be too careful and all the men were in the fields.

Her heart was beating rapidly as she went through the house, checking windows and doors. For herself Babette hoped that the visitors would be Cavaliers and be able to give them news of how the war went for King Charles. She had no doubts where her loyalty lay. Her beloved father would have offered his sword to the King had he not died of a virulent fever the previous winter.

Lord Harvey had been failing since his beloved wife's death three years previously, followed a year later by the disappearance of his son, John. John, who was now Lord Harvey—unless already dead—had left the house in a rage, having quarrelled with his father over a young woman.

Since the young woman in question had also disappeared that same night it was presumed that they had run off together. John did not know of his father's death because no one had any idea of his whereabouts to let him know the sad news.

Babette had cried herself to sleep on many nights, wondering if the brother she'd adored still lived. Alone in the castle, she'd written tearfully to her mother's sister and been invited to come and stay with her aunt and uncle for as long as she wished.

They were a kindly couple, though Babette thought her uncle rather sombre at times. Aunt Minnie seemed a little in awe of him, always reluctant to speak on any subject unless Sir Matthew had made his feelings known. They had one son, Robert, who was presently away at college.

Robert was studying with a view to entering the church. His father had a living in his gift and would bestow it on his son when the present incumbent retired in a year or so, once Robert had taken his vows. Angelina was but fourteen, three years and some months younger than Babette.

The castle of Haverston was currently being held for the King by the Earl of Carlton, a distant cousin of Babette's father. His Majesty had appointed him custodian of Lord Harvey's estate and Babette's own fortune, until she came of age and it was established whether John was alive or dead.

Babette had come to her aunt because she was lonely, but glancing down into the courtyard as a party of some fifteen or twenty men rode in, her heart caught. In that moment she almost wished she was safe in the castle, but then scolded herself for being a coward. They were but men after all, even though she thought, from their dress, they were too sober to be Cavaliers. A man in a dark coat and grey breeches seemed to be at their head, but he was wearing a hat with a wide brim and she was unable to see his face.

Having ensured that all the windows and doors were shut, Babette ran quickly down the stairs as someone knocked at the door. The knocking was loud and insistent, reverberating through the house. The servants had huddled together looking scared, and Aunt Minnie was holding Angelina's hand. Babette saw that her cousin was crying and went to her, putting an arm about her shoulder.

'They will not harm you,' she whispered. 'I dare say they have come for food and supplies.'

'Open this door in the name of Parliament,' a stern voice said. 'I had not expected this from Sir Matthew Graham. We come to ask for help, not as an enemy.'

Aunt Minnie's brow creased, a puzzled look in her eyes. 'I think I know that voice,' she said doubtfully. 'It may be your uncle's second cousin on his mother's side…Sir James Colby…'

'Should I ask him what he wants of us?'

Babette's aunt hesitated, but Babette did not wait. Going to the door, she called out in a loud voice, asking their visitor to give his name and state his business.

'We barred our doors, for we did not know who you were, sir,' she said. 'We are a house of women and dare not admit strangers in such fearful times.'

'Is that Lady Graham?'

'No, her niece, Mistress Harvey.'

'I am second cousin to Sir Matthew—and I come in friendship. My name is James Colby.'

'Open the door,' Aunt Minnie said, looking relieved. 'Sir James may enter, but his men must remain outside until my husband returns.'

Babette lifted the bar cautiously, peeping round the door. Her first glimpse was of a tall, commanding figure. The stranger had removed his hat, and she could see that he was dark-haired with eyes of grey, a firm hard chin and a mouth that at this moment looked stern and angry.

'My aunt says she will admit you, sir, but

your men must remain outside until my uncle returns.'

'They are tired and weary from the road, lady,' Sir James said with a sigh, his eyes narrowed and his manner harsh. 'It seems that this is Royalist territory, but I thought we would receive a better welcome from my cousin's house.'

Babette pushed a lock of pale hair back beneath the modest cap she was wearing. Despite his expression, she decided that the stranger looked more weary than dangerous and stood back to allow him to enter. Sympathy was in her voice as she said, 'If your men would care to go inside the barn and rest, I am sure we could send food and refreshments to them, sir.'

'Thank you, mistress,' Sir James said. His gaze focused on her for the first time and he made a jerky movement with his hand; for a moment the expression in his eyes made her fear, for it was such a strange, intense look he gave her, a flame deep in his eyes—but then he smiled. When he smiled it was as if he were a different man, his eyes almost silver and lit from within.

Babette's heart caught oddly, because his smile was most pleasant, even though he had confessed himself for Parliament and was therefore her enemy. He turned and directed his men towards the barn, and they dismounted leading their horses towards the shelter it offered.

'Sir James, forgive us,' Aunt Minnie said, coming forward. 'Sir Matthew has gone down to the long field to cut the wheat and most of the servants are with him. We were afraid of so large a party of men coming to the house and locked our doors. Will you not step into the parlour, sir? We shall give you food and drink, and my husband will be here shortly to speak with you himself.'

'Yes, thank you kindly, Lady Graham.' He had taken off his hat now, and Babette saw that his hair was longer than the style adopted by many of those who had joined the ranks of Parliament and were known as Puritans, because of their strict views on religion and private life. His clothes were of a sober hue, dark grey with a sash of yellow across his chest, a leather belt, which held a plain scabbard and his sword, gloves of buff leather and long black boots. His collar was white linen with a small edging of embroidery. Most men of the Puritan persuasion allowed themselves no ornament of any kind, perhaps to set themselves aside from the Cavaliers who delighted in finery and the latest fal-lals.

Hurrying to the kitchen, Babette spoke to Maria, arranging for food and drink to be carried to the men outside. She poured ale into a pewter jug, set fresh bread, a small crock of butter, cheese, a cold chop of pig meat and a bowl of her aunt's best pickles upon a tray, adding a slice of apple pie with cinnamon she'd made earlier that morning. Carrying it into the parlour where her aunt was still speaking with Sir Matthew's cousin, she set it down on the table.

His gaze went appreciatively over the food offered. 'You have been most generous, mistress. I thank you for your kindness. My men will be grateful for whatever you have. We have ridden for several days, finding food where we could. Since we encountered the enemy in a skirmish some days ago, we have been without some of our baggage. Some householders have been kind enough, but others made it clear we were not welcome.'

'We are at war, sir, and not everyone is of your persuasion. Some would feel you are rebels—traitors.' Babette had spoken without thinking and she saw the flash of fire in his eyes. She saw a nerve flick at his temple and his hands clenched. He was clearly angry, though he struggled to control it.

'The King is the traitor to his country,' he said harshly. 'It was he that imposed the tax of ship money on us, he that imposed the iniquitous Star Chamber—and he that tried to arrest the five members.'

'He tried to arrest them because they defied their King,' she replied, angry in her turn. Her head went up, and, had she known it, her eyes flashed in temper. 'If the King needs money for a war and the Parliament will not grant it, he must impose taxes whether they be popular or not…' She faltered as she saw the leap of answering fury in his eyes, then, aware that she had pushed him too far, said more hesitantly, 'That was my father's opinion…'

'Then he would be for the King,' Sir James said. 'I had thought this household for Parliament—am I wrong?'

'Take no notice of Babette,' Aunt Minnie said soothingly. 'She is but a girl and talks of what she does not understand. Sir Matthew, like many others, does not take one side or the

other, sir, but hopes only for peace—though
he will tell you himself, for here he comes.'

She breathed a sigh of relief as her husband
walked in and pushed Babette before her from
the room. Only when in the kitchen did she
speak to her niece.

'You should be more careful, Niece. I know
your father was a true Royalist and that may
be your persuasion, as it may be mine, but
we must keep silent, especially when there are
men of another persuasion in the house, dearest.'

'Yes, forgive me, Aunt. I should not have
spoken so to a guest, even if I was angered by
his views. It was rude and immodest of me.'

'Your uncle might think it immodest and
perhaps Sir James might find you impertinent,
but I do not blame you—though I caution you
not to speak so frankly before your uncle.'

'Forgive me. I do not know what made me
lose my temper.'

Yet she knew only too well. It was the man
with the eyes of cold steel who looked at her
so arrogantly that she had wanted to strike him
and had spoken thoughtlessly.

'You are entitled to your own views, Babette—but it is best not to speak them in Sir Matthew's house.'

'Is my uncle of their persuasion, Aunt?'

'I would not say that he was for Parliament. Sir Matthew is against any war that sets brother against brother and father against son. He cares for his land and would see it prosper. War is dangerous, Babette. Tempers rise and terrible things are said and done. As yet we have lived quietly here—but for how long can it continue? This is the first time soldiers have come to our door and they came in peace— but others may demand where Sir James requests. I think it will not be long before the whole country is aflame and then we shall all have to choose one way or the other.'

'Yes, I know, Aunt.' Babette was thoughtful. Her uncle had said little about the outcome of the first battle of the war at Edge Hill. The matter of who had won depended on whose side you supported, for some declared that it was a victory for the King, while others thought the men of Parliament might have won a decisive victory had they held on a little longer. In the months since that first battle there had been only minor skirmishes, indecisive clashes that had no real significance, small troops of opposing forces that met and fought. It had mainly been a time of recouping on both sides, of drawing lines and discovering who was your friend and who your enemy. 'I know the castle of Haverston still stands for the King, but some houses are not as well defended and have fallen to the rebels.'

'You ought not to name them so,' her aunt chided her gently. 'It shows your loyalty and may make you enemies. Sir Matthew has been careful not to choose sides publicly, though I think perhaps he may be drawn more to the side of Parliament, for he says they are the voice of the people.'

'Surely his Majesty speaks for the people?' Babette was puzzled. 'Does the King not rule by divine right?'

'It is certainly the King's opinion and that of his followers,' her aunt replied, 'but I am not sure. Your uncle is not against the King. Far from it—but he would have his Majesty rule by the consent of the people.' Lady Graham sighed. 'Yes, I know, dearest, it is a puzzle to me, too. I know not what to think.'

Babette made no reply. Her uncle was a studious man and he often lectured them about

theology and, it seemed, the rights of kings—
at least he had confided these views to his wife.

She could not know whether her uncle was
right or wrong. Certainly, she agreed with him
that war was unfortunate. She'd heard that in
some parts of the country marauding soldiers
of either persuasion had commandeered grain,
cattle and horses, leaving the owners without payment and in fear of their lives. Some
who had fought for their possessions were left
wounded or dying; it was indeed a bitter conflict that turned families against one another
and set neighbours at war with each other.

'I shall try to be careful, Aunt,' she promised, 'for I do not wish to bring trouble upon
you and your family.'

'I know that, dearest,' Lady Graham said.
'You have been a joy to me since you came
here. Your cousin is still a young girl, though
she does not like it to be said. I have found your
company comforting, and you have helped me
in so many ways. I should be loath to part from
you—if your uncle decided that it was not suitable for you to remain here.'

It was the implication, the words left unsaid,
that shocked her.

Would her uncle banish her to the castle?

Babette's heart sank. She much preferred life in this comfortable manor house to that in the bleak and often icy cold castle. The discomfort had never bothered her when her parents lived and her brother was at home, but without them it had become a lonely place indeed and she had no wish to return. Her days had been busy at the castle, but the nights were long and gave her too much time to remember and regret. She would take her aunt's warning seriously and watch her tongue, especially when her uncle was near.

Babette wondered if the Parliament man would complain of her to his cousin. As she helped Aunt Minnie wash and preserve the plums she'd picked earlier in the huge iron pan of sugar syrup, she contemplated the idea of being banished to her home. She would miss her aunt and her cousin very much. Hearing the heavy tread of her uncle's step, she tensed, fearing his anger. However, when he entered the kitchen he was smiling.

'Ah, there you are, Babette,' he said, 'helping your aunt like the good girl you are. Would you take more ale to the parlour, please? I have invited Sir James to stay with us for a few days. His men are on a mission to purchase cattle and horses and I have told him that I will help him, though I will not have my neighbours robbed.'

'Will they sell to Parliament forces?' Babette said and wished she had not as she saw her uncle frown. 'Forgive me, Uncle. It is not my place to question.'

'It was a pertinent question, Niece,' he said and sighed heavily. 'Because of our relationship, Sir James is willing to bargain for what he wants—though I fear that others may not be so nice. Both sides are taking what they want, Babette. If we wish to survive and see our neighbours prosper as we do ourselves, we must tread carefully.'

'Yes, sir. I understand that,' she replied. Her uncle was sometimes stern and sombre, but she saw that he was a good man at heart. He had not chosen to fight and some might look askance at him for that, but she knew that all he wished for was a quiet life in which to nurture his land, care for his family and be on good terms with his neighbours—but for how long would he be allowed to live as he preferred?

Babette picked up a jug of ale and went back to the parlour, hearing her aunt and uncle begin

to talk in low voices as she closed the door.
She'd feared that their visitor might have complained of her, but it was obvious that he had
not for her uncle was not cross with her. He
was generous at times, but also superstitious
and often stern. He would have no mistletoe
or greenery in the house at Christmas for it
was a pagan custom and, he said, a tool of the
Devil, the custom of kissing beneath a bough
immodest.

Sir James was standing by the window,
looking out into the garden as she approached.
His view was of a small courtyard garden
set with flowers of all kinds: damask roses,
zdaisies, the remains of the gillyflowers, lilies
and sweet-scented stocks, which were fodder
for the bees that lived in their hives and supplied them with wonderful honey.

'Your ale, sir.' Babette set down her tray and
was about to move away when he turned and
looked at her. For a moment she was shocked
by the haunted expression in his eyes and once
again her heart caught. He looked so grief-
stricken and for a moment she saw a different
man. What could have caused that look?

'Who tends your garden, mistress?'

'I do most of it, though Jonas helps me when I need some heavy digging.'

'Your hives do well?'

'Yes, sir. Very well.' She poured some ale into his cup, noticing that he had eaten most of the food she'd brought for him. 'Have you eaten sufficient?'

'Quite sufficient, mistress. My compliments to your aunt—that apple pie was delicious.'

'I made it…' Babette said and then blushed, for he would think she was asking for praise. 'My mother taught me. She was a wonderful cook—and my aunt likes me to make pies for her.'

'I see…' There was a faint smile in his eyes now. 'Is your mother dead, mistress?'

'Yes, sir, these three years past of a fever.'

'And your father?'

'He died last year. I came to live here with my aunt because it was lonely without them.'

'Sir Matthew tells me that your brother is Lord Harvey—but none knows if he lives?' Sir James looked at her curiously. 'Is your uncle your guardian?'

'Nay, sir. His Majesty appointed the Earl of Carlton the custodian of the castle and my portion. I suppose either he or the King himself would be my guardian until my brother can be traced.'

'Ah…' He nodded, frowning again. 'So that is where your Royalist persuasion came from. I thought it odd, for my cousin is surely of a different persuasion, even though he chooses not to take up arms.'

His eyes were cold as they went over her and yet a fire seemed to leap at their heart. Babette's stomach clenched, for this man affected her more than she cared to admit. He was arrogant and an enemy, and this feeling in her stomach must be fear, though she was not usually so easily intimidated. Yet what else could cause her to tremble inwardly?

Babette set her lips primly. It was not for her to say why her uncle had not chosen for one side or the other. Her uncle's views were his and he had no doubt made as much known to his cousin as he wished.

'You are not betrothed?' Sir James asked, bringing a betraying flush to her cheeks. 'Your uncle said it had not yet been thought of.'

'I see no reason why you should wish to know that,' Babette said, raised to a quick anger by his impertinence. He had no right to question her on such a subject. 'My father was to have arranged a betrothal just before he died—to Andrew Melbourne.'

'Lord Melbourne's son?' His gaze narrowed. 'Drew is my cousin once removed. I descended through the female line, but one of my ancestors was a Melbourne—her name was Catherine. Drew was once my good friend, but we have not spoken since before the Battle of Edge Hill. I regret the breach, for we were once good friends, but it was inevitable.'

'Drew is for the King, of course.' Babette's head went up, her stance certain and proud.

'Yes.' Sir James looked at her, a brooding expression in his eyes. 'Have you heard from him since your father died?'

'No.' Babette licked her lips nervously. It was one of the reasons she had cried herself to sleep each night before she came here. Although she had only met the handsome young man once, she had been excited by the thought of marrying him. She had thought he would come to the castle to claim her when he heard of her father's death, but he had not. Indeed, she'd heard nothing of him since that date and supposed that he considered himself free to marry where he chose, since the betrothal had not actually happened.

'I thought not,' James said, a strange look in his eyes. She thought that he had more to say, but withheld it for some reason of his own. If he had news of Drew, in his arrogance he would not tell her. 'Thank you for your ale, mistress. Your uncle has said that I may use the blue chamber while we stay here. I trust my presence in the house will not cause you sleepless nights?'

'Should it?' She frowned at him, annoyed that she had told him more than she'd intended of her life. He was an enemy and nothing to her, nor could he ever be. 'I see no reason why your presence should make any difference to my life.'

'Indeed, it should not,' he replied, a smile playing across his mouth. She wondered why her eyes were drawn to his mouth. It was not as if he was likely to kiss her. Why had that thought entered her mind? Babette was horrified. She did not wish any man to kiss her unless he was her husband—and she certainly would not wish to marry a Puritan, though perhaps this man was more a soldier than a man of religious fervour.

This was ridiculous! Her heart was racing

wildly and her cheeks burned as the foolish thoughts chased through her mind.

Babette withdrew her eyes hurriedly, collecting the empty plates and jug on to her tray. She picked it up and left before he could speak again. He had gone back to his contemplation of the garden and she sensed a heaviness in his mood that intrigued her.

Why should the contemplation of her garden make him sad? She was sure that he hid a secret sorrow behind that mask of indifference but could not imagine what it was—or why her garden should remind him.

James continued to gaze into the garden after the girl had left him. His mind was confused, for on first seeing her something had arrested his speech, suspending his thought for an instant that seemed like an aeon of time, and taking his breath. What it was about the young woman that should render him so he could not tell. He had believed he could never feel any true human emotion again, certainly not the softer feelings that he'd known when his sweet Jane was alive.

Surely he could not be attracted to a woman he had met only this day? No, it was foolish, ridiculous…a betrayal of Jane. And yet there had been something the moment he saw her, and, as he'd watched her working, his first feeling had not been reversed that here was a remarkable young woman.

A woman who might help him to live again, perhaps?

Even as the thought entered his mind, he crushed it ruthlessly, a wave of such intense grief sweeping through him that he gasped. What a rogue he was to contemplate caring for a woman when his beloved lay in her grave.

'Forgive me, Jane,' he whispered. 'I shall never love any other woman, for you were my heart and my soul.'

In time he might marry, for a man could not live his life alone, but he would choose a widow who wanted only a home and comfort. He could not give more…even to the girl whose eyes had seemed to pierce the shield he had built to shut out his grief and despair.

Chapter Two

Babette glanced out of the kitchen window, though she was not precisely sure what she sought or why. Captain Colby, for such his men called him, had been out with her uncle and half of his men all that afternoon. As she stood at the window, she saw they were returning, her uncle and the rebel captain riding side by side as they entered the courtyard. One of the men was driving a wagon filled with sacks and leading two bullocks at the back of the cart. Clearly their expedition had been successful, though she could see no sign of the horses they needed, but then, most of the neighbouring farms had only the horses they used for riding or work in the fields. Her father had kept a fine stable at the castle, but Babette had brought only her favourite mare when she'd come to the manor house.

As she watched, Captain Colby dismounted, and a servant took his horse. He glanced towards the kitchen, as if seeking something, and Babette's heart leapt. How foolish! He did not look for her. Why should he? Besides, she did not wish him to notice her. He was too arrogant—her enemy.

She and her aunt had been busy baking all the afternoon, for with so many extra guests they would need to provide more bread and pies if they were to feed hungry men. Angelina had made some custard tarts, but her task was mainly peeling and chopping the vegetables that would go into the stewpot. The big black pot hung on a tripod over an open fire and the main ingredient in this night's meal was mutton, cooked long and slow to make it tender, with bacon, onions, dried beans, herbs, carrots, leeks and turnips, cooked out to add thickness to the gravy. Also large dumplings made from flour and suet, which were filling and would satisfy hungry men.

Babette had sipped the gravy and she knew that the food tasted delicious. In winter she would also have added potatoes to the mix towards the end of the cooking time, but their stores of those precious roots had been used before the spring was out and there would be no more until the next harvest this autumn.

For pudding there were stewed plums she had picked that day from the orchard, custard, pastries sweetened with honey and a quince preserve. Besides these dishes there would be fresh bread, butter and soft white cheese from their own cows. It was truly a feast fit for any man. Aunt Minnie bemoaned the fact that she had no pig pies or trotters to offer as delicacies, but Sir Matthew never killed a pig unless there was an R in the month, for the meat would spoil too soon.

Glancing through the small-paned kitchen window again, Babette saw the rebel captain washing his face and hands beneath the pump before turning to walk up to the house. She averted her head quickly, her heart's strident beat bringing a flush to her cheeks. Rather than let him think she had been watching him, she loaded a tray with bread, cheese and butter and took it through to the parlour, setting it on a side table of oak. Earlier, Angelina had laid places on the long refectory table for the

family, their female servants, Jonas and the
captain.

Babette straightened a chair, casting her eye
over the fare laid out. The cold food would be
close at hand and either she or her aunt would
serve the men with the hot dishes before sitting themselves, while the servants waited to
serve themselves once the family were seated.
Babette had found her uncle's habit of eating
at the same table as his servants odd at first,
for her father's hall was much larger than this
parlour and though everyone ate in the same
room there was a distance between the lord
and his followers. However, she was not at the
castle. She had grown used to supping with the
servants, but fervently hoped that she would
not be seated next to their guest. The less she
had to do with him the better. He had a way of
looking at her that made her stomach clench
and might make it impossible for her to eat
her meal.

However, Aunt Minnie had other ideas and
she directed the stranger to take the seat of
honour, next to her husband and therefore on
Babette's right hand. He politely stood until
she sat, pulling out her stool so that she could
take her place. Only her aunt and uncle had

chairs with backs, another thing that had taken some getting used to when she first came here. At the castle she had a chair of her own, with a straight plain back and two arms to place her elbows. In her bedchamber, her chair had cushions she had embroidered herself, but her father would have thought it too soft to use at table, for one sat up straight to eat and did not slouch.

Babette saw the stranger frown as he realised that she had a stool, as of course he did since there were no other chairs. Perhaps he was not used to using them and felt discomfort in the arrangement?

Her uncle said grace as usual. Aunt Minnie rose after grace had been said and fetched the large tureen of stew from the side table, which she ladled into earthenware dishes for the men, before serving Babette, her daughter and herself. Babette offered bread to everyone, and Maria poured ale into mugs. Sir Matthew seldom had wine at table, for it was mostly sour and needed to be sweetened with honey, unless they were fortunate to have French wine, which tasted smoother. Good wine was expensive and saved for times of celebration and the family drank Aunt Minnie's homebrewed ale. This evening, though, a rough red wine was offered to their guest, and Sir Matthew drank wine himself, though both Babette and her aunt preferred the weak ale they normally drank.

As she retook her seat, Captain Colby stood once more, insisting on placing her chair for her. Babette's cheeks flushed; he was their guest and should not wait on her, but as she looked at her uncle she saw approval in his eyes. Feeling the flutter in her lower stomach, Babette murmured her thanks, but avoided the soldier's eyes.

Taking her seat once more, Babette looked down at her trencher. She was very conscious of the man sitting beside her and noticed that he merely sipped his wine and then reached for the glass of fresh spring water that one of the women had placed for him. They were fortunate in having such pure water from their own spring. In towns and cities, Babette had heard it was dangerous to drink the water, for it was often contaminated, but theirs was pure and sweet and she saw the appreciation in the way their guest drank deeply of his.

'You do not drink wine, mistress?' he asked as he saw her sip her ale and then the water.

'I prefer a sweeter variety than my uncle's cellar can provide, sir.'

He nodded, and she thought that perhaps he felt the same, though would not say. 'Your aunt's home brew is most pleasant to the taste.'

'Yes, sir. Like the water it has been cooled, for Aunt Minnie considers it more palatable thus.'

Again he nodded, as if agreeing. She knew that her aunt kept a good table and no one could object to the food, but her uncle was careful with his silver and would not pay the high price many wine merchants asked for the sweet French wines.

'Did you have a good day, sir?' she asked out of a need to make conversation. He turned his sombre gaze on her, and she felt her throat catch under his dark scrutiny.

'We made some purchases, but hardly enough for our needs. We require much more flour and certainly more pigs and cattle, but your uncle's friends had little to spare. We were not offered one horse.'

'Perhaps in a few weeks when the harvest is gathered there will be more, sir. I fear there are few spare horses—but perhaps later this year if the travelling people bring their horses to the fair. Sometimes they have pure Arab bloodstock, but whether they would part with them is uncertain.'

'Yes. I believe the fairs would be the best source in normal times, but the travelling folk are avoiding the fairs now that the country is at war, I think.' He looked grim. 'It was my hope and that of some others that we might retain the goodwill of the landowners and farmers by buying produce, but if we are offered so little...'

Babette felt a tingle of alarm as he left the rest unsaid. She had heard that in some parts marauding soldiers had stolen cattle and grain, burning what still stood in the fields as a punishment to those who resisted. But the tales were vague and it had not happened here as yet.

'If Parliament is for the right of the people, how can you justify taking what people have toiled all year to produce without payment?'

'That is precisely my argument, mistress,' he replied and smiled at her in a way that had her tingling right down to her toes. 'An army must be fed and there are those who say we must take what we need if we cannot persuade.

However, for myself I shall also give payment where payment is due.'

Babette could not fault his reasoning, though she knew that most of the small farmers who helped her uncle to gather his harvest, and whom Sir Matthew helped in return, would produce only enough to feed themselves and their people throughout the year. The large landowners might have surplus corn, but hardly anyone had much to spare. Perhaps if the trees were laden with apples they might take some baskets to market, but as far as the grain, cows and pigs were concerned they raised only enough for their own needs. In times when the harvest was generally poor there was often not enough to go round and the poorest families might go hungry through the winter.

Sir Matthew had a large flock of geese, also several ducks and chickens. He did sometimes give a goose to a neighbour at Christmas and sometimes at that time of year he killed perhaps ten of his flock and took them to the market, but even if the rebels took the whole flock it would hardly be enough to feed the number of men she'd heard had rushed to join the Parliament's army.

'Some of our men have gone home to harvest their fields,' Captain Colby was speaking to Sir Matthew now, leaving Babette to her thoughts. 'It is necessary work, for if the wheat and oats were left to rot in the fields their families might starve, but it does not please Cromwell.'

'Is Cromwell not a farmer himself?'

'Aye, he is that, but he will not release the men who follow him this year and insists the women and old men, children and the infirm must gather in the harvest.'

'His attitude must be much resented?' Babette suggested.

He turned to look at her, his quiet grey eyes thoughtful. 'Perhaps by some, but he is admired and respected, some say loved, by the army. He speaks of more discipline needed amongst the ranks and of turning his men into battle-ready troops rather than a disorganised rabble.'

'I do not know the man,' Sir Matthew said. 'I believe he lives in Cambridgeshire? Here in Sussex his name has reached us, though as yet we have seen little of your fellow officers, Colby.'

'Do you intend to stay long, sir?' Babette

asked when her uncle had turned to speak to Jonas.

'A few more days. I should like at least two cartloads of grain and another six or more cattle to send back to the quartermaster before I move on to the next location. Since your uncle has kindly offered us a place to sleep, we have decided to make our headquarters here while we see what is on offer to us.'

A few more days... she thought.

Babette nodded, but made no reply. She had no right to resent her uncle's decision, for it was his house, but she wished that he had not made the rebels so welcome. She was tempted to return to the castle, but knew that she would find it lonely. Before the rebels came, she had allowed herself to forget the war and believed that her aunt had a softness for the Royal cause, but her uncle had now made his true colours known. He had not chosen to fight, but he was making his home available for the Parliament men; he had effectively made his choice, even though he would not take up his sword.

Her feelings must have shown themselves somehow for she was aware that he looked at her with some amusement.

'Yes, you must put up with me a little longer. Fear not, lady. I shall not demand that you put away your finery and wear plain black. I am not a Puritan, though I fight side by side with them.'

Babette glared at him. Why did he find the situation amusing?

'If you are not of their persuasion, why do you take arms against the King?'

'I am for the people. I would have the King rule, but by consent of people and Parliament, not as the autocrat he believes his divine right gives him the authority to be.'

His beliefs were much as her uncle's. Her uncle's views had not concerned Babette one way or the other—so why then did she feel such a strong aversion to this man?

She averted her gaze and saw that her aunt was signalling to her. Getting up from the table, she fetched bread, butter, tarts and cheese to set before the men. The servants had begun to clear the dirty trenchers and were now replenishing ale, water and wine. After she had finished her task, Babette took her seat once more, sliding quickly into place before Captain Colby had more than half-risen from his seat.

'You need not rise for me, sir,' she said

softly. 'Here in my uncle's house all the women wait at table.'

'A custom I am unused to,' he murmured softly. 'In my house a gentleman stands for a lady.'

Babette smiled. 'As in my father's house, but we are all equal in the sight of the Lord—so my uncle says.'

'Yes. While I agree, there are differences…'

In her heart Babette knew that her father and brother would agree with him, but here in this house they lived by Sir Matthew's rules. She arched her brows at him as if to imply she disapproved of his sentiments, but knew she did it only because she had to protect herself from him. His chivalry and charm must not be allowed to breech her defences. No matter if she liked his smile, he was an enemy of all that she believed in. She must always be on her guard.

Now why did she feel she needed protection from him? He was a gentleman and a guest in her uncle's house. She was certain he would not abuse Sir Matthew's hospitality—so why did she feel she needed to keep a barrier between them?

* * *

Babette was relieved when at last her aunt signalled that they were to clear the dishes to the kitchen and leave the men to talk business over their ale. Babette carried a loaded tray to the door. Usually, she set it down on a small table, but before she could do so Captain Colby had opened the door for her, holding it as she and then Maria passed through. She gave him a small smile and a faint shake of her head, but his expression did not change and he continued to hold the door as her aunt followed with another loaded tray.

Babette was already at the sink, beginning to pour a kettle filled with hot water over the greasy plates. She added a liquid soap her aunt made herself and was about to start washing dishes when her aunt stopped her.

'Let Maria do that, Babette. You do not want to make your hands red. Captain Colby might notice and he treats you as a lady, as I suppose you are.' Aunt Minnie was looking faintly troubled. 'When you came here your uncle expected you to live as we do, Babette— but your father was Lord Harvey and perhaps I was wrong to allow it.'

'Do not be foolish, dearest Aunt,' Babette

said. 'I like to help you. Pray ignore Captain Colby. His manners are good, but while I am in your home I do not consider myself above you or my uncle.'

'Your uncle's views are not shared by everyone,' Aunt Minnie said. 'You will leave the dishes to Maria, please, and return to the parlour. You may sit and sew and listen to the gentlemen talk.'

'And leave all the work to you and Maria?' Babette frowned. 'No, certainly not. If I may not wash the dishes, I shall dry them and put them away. It is you who should be sitting in the parlour with my uncle and his guest.'

Aunt Minnie looked at her doubtfully. 'Captain Colby...' She sighed and shook her head. 'I would not wish to spoil your chances of a good marriage, Babette. My sister looked much higher than I and found herself a rich lord. Matthew was enough for me, but I was never as beautiful as your mama, dearest.'

Babette acknowledged that her aunt was homely rather than beautiful, but she was a kind, gentle lady and she was angry that the rebel captain had put such doubts into her mind.

'You need not concern yourself on my account, Aunt. I would never marry a rebel—and I do not care for Captain Colby. I find him arrogant and...' Her words died on her lips as the door opened and she saw him standing there. He had carried Greta's tray for her, perhaps considering it too heavy for the elderly servant.

While Babette's cheeks burned, for he could not have failed to hear her comment, Lady Graham bustled forward, begging him to set down the tray and return to the parlour.

'You should not, sir. It is not a gentleman's place to carry for a servant.'

'She is also a woman and elderly. She looked to be in need of help, so I offered. I beg you, do not scold Greta, ma'am.'

'No, I shall not,' she said and looked flustered. 'But I beg you not to tarry. You must have more important things... Sir Matthew will want to discuss your business...'

'I shall not keep him waiting a moment longer.' Captain Colby glanced at Babette, his eyes so cold and icy that she knew he'd heard her and was angry. He inclined his head, his silence speaking volumes as he left them.

'Do you think he heard what you said?'

Babette raised her head as she answered her

aunt, 'I care not what he heard. He means nothing to me nor ever could.'

'He lives in a much bigger house than ours,' Aunt Minnie said. 'I believe his family to be wealthy—and they have been influential at court in the past. I must confess I was surprised to see that he was one of the…one of the Parliament men. I had thought he would offer his sword to the King.'

'He says his Majesty is unjust and must come to terms with his Parliament and rule by consent of the people.'

'Yes, in that I cannot fault him. But the King is…' She shook her head and sighed. 'We must not worry our heads over such things, my love. Your uncle knows what is best and we must abide by his wishes.'

Aunt Minnie was so submissive to her husband's wishes, never venturing a contrary opinion, at least in Babette's hearing. If every woman was expected to behave so meekly, perhaps Babette would do well to remain unwed.

She sighed inwardly as she finished stacking the dried dishes, then struck a tinder and lit a taper, holding it to her chamberstick.

'I shall retire for the night, Aunt.'

'It is early yet,' Aunt Minnie said. 'Why

do you not sit in the parlour and listen to your uncle and his guest? Sir Matthew will expect it.'

'Pray tell my uncle I have the headache and ask him to forgive me,' Babette said. She kissed her aunt's cheek and picked up her chamberstick, leaving the kitchen before Aunt Minnie could object.

Alone in her room, Babette went to sit on the deep windowsill and look out at the night. It was a clear, still night and over-warm, the room so stuffy that she opened the casement to catch a breath of air. As she did so, she caught sight of something in the bushes. Her room overlooked the kitchen gardens, and she was not sure whether she'd seen a man's figure or not. Was it one of the servants—or perhaps one of Captain Colby's men?

'Babette—is that you?'

The sibilant whisper was just beneath her window. She leaned forward and saw the man hiding behind the water butt. Immediately, her heart caught with fright and then started thumping madly as she saw who it was.

'John—is that you?' she called. 'Is it truly you come home?'

'Shush,' the voice said in a harsh whisper. 'I've seen horses—they belong to the rebels we've been following. Are they in the house?'

'Yes, their captain is,' she said, leaning out of her window to look down at him. 'His men are in the barn—nearly twenty of them. If you are for the King, you must be careful.'

'Can you help us? We need food and water—and a horse. Drew's was shot from under him and he has a wound himself.'

'Do you recall when we stayed here once as children?'

'Yes...' John sounded hesitant, then, 'The hut we played in, in the woods—is it still there?'

'Take your friend there,' Babette said. 'I will go down as soon as the others have retired and bring you food and ale.'

'Can you not come down now?'

'I shall try,' she said. 'Hide in the shrubbery and I will see if I can find anything left from supper.'

Blowing out her chamberstick, Babette left her chamber and crept back down the stairs to the kitchen. She listened for a moment then, deciding it was quiet, went in. Aunt Minnie must have sent the servants to bed or perhaps on an errand, and she herself was probably in the parlour.

Seeing the remains of a loaf, a heel of cheese and the remainder of a quince tart she'd made, she gathered them into a muslin bag, then picked up a quartern pot of ale and approached the back door. She found it locked and was in the act of turning the key when the door opened and Greta entered.

'Where be you going, Mistress Babette?'

'I need a little air, my head aches…' Babette saw her looking at the food. 'I'm hungry. I couldn't eat at table. Please do not tell my aunt.'

Greta smiled, revealing her toothless grin. She went to the table and picked up a slice of pie. 'I shan't tell if you don't…' she cackled and, tucking the pie into her apron pocket, she went back into the hall.

Babette smiled to herself as she left the house and began to walk towards the shrubbery. That was not the first time Greta had returned to the kitchen to steal an extra slice of pie when her mistress was otherwise engaged. Aunt Minnie knew she did it and laughed to Babette, for as she said she did not grudge her servants their food and the old woman might have asked for it, but preferred to raid the kitchen when others were in bed.

Reaching the spot where she'd seen her brother hide, Babette was about to call out when she felt herself caught from behind and a hand went over her mouth.

'Be careful, Babs, those devils are everywhere. Give me the food and go back to the house quickly before they wonder what you are doing.'

No one had called her Babs since her brother disappeared and she felt the tears spring to her eyes as she said, 'Where have you been?'

'In Holland. I came to England with Prince Rupert to fight for the King. What are you doing here in a house of rebels?'

'My uncle is not a rebel. He has not taken sides, at least until now—but the rebel captain is a second cousin. They are looking for grain and cattle and will stay here for a few days.'

'God rot them,' John said angrily. 'I had hoped we might find a place to rest here. Drew is wounded and needs to rest. We were six of us on a similar mission to your rebel captain when a larger party set upon us. Four of my friends were killed. Drew and I escaped and came here.'

'Take your friend to the hut... Wait.' Babette bent down and quickly pulled off her linen petticoat, giving it to him. 'There is a stream nearby where you can find water to drink. Use this linen to bind his wound. Tomorrow I will make a salve and bring it with more food. I shall tell Aunt Minnie I am going foraging for herbs and roots—and I shall do so, but first I will bring the things you need.'

'Thank you, Sister,' John said and smiled at her. 'I'd heard you were here. I am glad to find you well.'

'Have you been home?'

'I know Father is dead. I told the King I would rather be free to fight with the prince than be cooped up in the castle. Lord Carlton will continue to hold it for us—and you should return home, Babette. I shall visit you there and bring Alice to you.'

'Alice...your wife?'

John's face relaxed into a smile that softened his features. 'My Alice is with child. She begged me to keep her with me, and I did at the start, but now she is six months gone and cannot travel fast. I have sent her to the castle for her own safety—but you must promise me to join her. You will, won't you, Babs?'

Babette thought regretfully of her aunt's warm kitchen and her kindness, but her duty was clear.

'Yes, of course, I shall now that I know you are alive and that you have a wife who needs me. I shall tell Aunt Minnie tomorrow, but it may be a few days before I can leave. Uncle Matthew may not be able to spare anyone to bring me home because of the harvest. I should need to travel with just Jonas as my escort.'

'Once your rebels have gone, I shall come to the house and fetch you,' John said. 'I must go now, for Drew needs my help. Be careful, Babs—and tell no one that you've seen me while the rebels are in the house.'

'No, of course not. God be with you, Brother.'

Babette had given him all the food she'd brought. She stood watching as he melted away into the shadows. Then she turned and started to walk back to the house. As she approached the kitchen door, a shadow moved towards her, making her jump.

'Did I startle you, mistress?'

Captain Colby's voice was somehow reassuring, though her heart beat wildly. Somehow she would rather it was he than one of his men—but what had he seen? What did he know?

'Good even', sir. I thought you with my uncle in the parlour?'

'He had some business with one of his tenants—and I came out for a little air.'

'As I did,' Babette said and tried to pass him, but his hand shot out, imprisoning her wrist. His fingers seemed to hold her lightly, but in a grip she could not break and her heart was beating like a drum. 'I pray you, let me go, sir. I would go in…'

'Who were you speaking with just now?' She could hear the suspicion in his tone and feared that he had seen too much.

Babette's heart was racing. John had warned her to tell no one that she'd seen him and she certainly would not tell this man the truth. John had a friend he called Drew and his friend had been injured in a fight with the rebels, four of his friends already dead. The Parliament men were her enemies and she had no wish to speak with this man. Yet if she denied speaking with someone he would know she was lying and think the worst.

Lifting her head, she looked him in the eyes.

'I do not see it is your business, sir—but I was meeting a friend, a man I care for.'

'Ah, your lover...' Captain Colby's eyes narrowed, and she thought he looked angry. 'Does your aunt know that you sneak out late at night to seek your lover? No? I thought not. Your uncle would not care for it, I think. He is a strict man and might forbid you his house.'

'I intend to return home soon,' Babette said, stung to anger. He would think her immodest now and for some reason that hurt and shamed her, but to tell him the truth would cause trouble for her brother and his friend.

'You might have no choice if your uncle had caught you.'

'As I said, it is none of your affair. I am naught to you, sir.'

'No, but you might have been. I had it in mind to ask your uncle for you in marriage... but I do not care for tainted goods.' There was a note of anger or perhaps disappointment in his voice as he suddenly let her go and swung away from her.

Babette caught her breath as he left her standing there. How dare he say such a thing! He was impertinent, arrogant. She would never have agreed to such a match. How could he even think it? Besides, her hand was not in her uncle's giving, though of course her uncle might claim he had as much right as the guardian appointed by the King. Neither he nor this impossible man knew that her brother lived.

Her brother lived. Warmth soothed away the anger as she dwelled on the happy news that John was alive and here in England, fighting with the King's troops. She smiled as she went back into the house, lit another candle and carried it upstairs to her chamber.

This time she drew her curtains and undressed, feeling ready for bed. Even though she soon drifted into sleep her rest was disturbed by strange dreams. However, when she woke they melted with the sunshine of another day.

Meanwhile, James walked on into the darkness, needing as he so often did the solitude that night provided. His thoughts were tormented, for though he could forget his grief for a time, losing himself in duty, when his work was done his thoughts turned always to the woman he'd loved so dearly.

His grief had lived with him for months, yet as he walked alone and looked at the stars, he could not banish the expression in the young woman's eyes when he'd accosted her. She was startled, almost guilty. He'd accused her of having a lover. She had not completely denied it, though seemed outraged at the suggestion.

Why had he told her that it had been in his mind to ask her uncle for her? Had he wanted to punish her for being less than he'd thought her at the start? What had made him strike out like that?

Was she a girl of low morals? Despite finding her in such a compromising position, he did not believe her immodest.

Then why had she been outside and why did she not wish to speak of her reasons for being there? Was she meeting someone who would not wish to be seen by him?

Had she met a Royalist? In secret so that her uncle should not know?

The thought sent a shiver down his spine, for it would make her a traitor in his eyes... and yet, perversely, he did not wish to lose his good opinion of her. For some obscure reason, he would prefer that she had Royalist friends rather than her having been in the arms of a lover.

What was it to him what the girl did? James

swore beneath his breath. She was but a chance acquaintance, someone he would never meet again. If he wished to wed, surely any gentle, obliging woman would serve his needs?

He had not looked at a woman and thought of marriage once in the months since Jane died. Why now? What was it about this woman that had made him suddenly stir to anger because she was willing to give herself so carelessly?

Damn him for a fool! He cared not what she had been doing. No woman could ever touch his heart again…and yet he would prefer to keep his good opinion of Miss Babette.

Chapter Three

'It is a lovely day,' Babette said when her aunt entered the kitchen and discovered her packing her basket. 'I am going to make the most of it by picking herbs and fungi.'

'What a good idea,' Aunt Minnie said. 'I would send Angelina with you, but she has the toothache. However, you may take Jonas if you wish.'

'Yes, Aunt, thank you.'

Babette had known she would not be permitted to go without a servant, but Jonas had come to the manor with her. He was primarily her groom, but did any other jobs that were needed about the house. Babette could be certain of his loyalty, for she knew he would never betray her no matter what she did.

'We shall not take the horses, for it is a nice

day for a walk—besides, there may be other soldiers looking for horses. I do not wish my mare to be stolen, and it would be wiser to leave her here,' Babette said. 'We shall be home in time to help you prepare supper, Aunt.'

'Enjoy yourself, dearest. You have taken some food to eat while you forage?'

'Yes, thank you.' Babette could scarcely conceal her flush, for she had taken enough to feed two hungry men. Aunt Minnie was certain to wonder at how much cheese and bread had gone from her shelves, though perhaps she would think it had been given to the soldiers in the barn.

Babette had been up at first light to begin the baking, and several loaves were already in the oven, waiting for her aunt to take them out. She had also made pies and tarts, which would take their turn in the oven when the bread was done. Even her uncle could not accuse her of shirking her work.

Before she began the baking, she had prepared a pot of salve and linen bandages. Besides the food, she had a sack of ale as well as a pewter bowl so that she could dip the cloth in cooling water; she would carry the water from the stream if John's friend was still in pain and needed her attentions.

She walked quickly towards the hut in the woods, Jonas following a few steps behind. Stopping every now and then to pick something she saw in the bushes, she looked back to see if she was followed. At the stream she filled the flask she'd slung from her chatelaine. Once she heard a twig crack and waited, but then a shy deer emerged from the thicket, looked at her, sniffed the air and bounded away. Babette smiled. The red deer here were safe enough, for though they belonged to the common forest and were no one man's property—not even in this case the King's, as were most of the deer in the country—they were seldom hunted at this time of year. Only in the winter did the landowners kill venison for their table and they usually agreed to take only a certain number so that the stocks would flourish. Poachers were not encouraged, though occasionally Sir Matthew would complain that it was happening and sometimes an example would be made, the poacher caught and punished by hanging.

When they approached the hut, Babette looked back again, making quite certain that she had not been followed. Telling her servant to wait for her and to keep a sharp lookout, she ran towards the hut. Jonas had raised his brows at her, but he had not questioned her. Reaching the woodsman's hut, she knocked softly and called out, then pushed open the door and entered. At once she saw that John was kneeling by the side of his friend, who was clearly ill. He cried out in his fever and threw out his arms, tears upon his face, as he called to someone called Beth.

Babette knelt beside him, placing a cool hand on his brow. He was burning hot and, as she looked at his shoulder, she saw the reason. John had removed his friend's shirt, and his shoulder was open to the air. Where the flesh had been laid open by a sword blade the wound was red and angry, a thick yellow pus oozing from the deep gash.

'How long has he been this way?' she asked as she poured water into her bowl from the flask she had filled at the stream. She took linen and began to bathe the inflamed flesh, gently probing and squeezing to make the pus come away from under the hard crust that had begun to form. Her patient screamed out in agony as she did so, making John look at her.

'Have a care, Babs. You are hurting him.'

'I know, but the wound must be cleansed,' she said patiently. 'I know because I've seen Mama do it when one of the men sliced into his leg with a scythe. I must wash away the pus and dirt and then apply salves. I wish I had something for his fever, but I had nothing to make the mixture with. I shall gather the herbs and leaves today and tomorrow I will bring him a drink that will ease him.'

'If he lasts the night,' John said. 'Lord Melbourne will be sorely distressed if his heir dies of a fever. He did not wish Drew to join the King, but there was no stopping him.'

'He is Drew Melbourne?' Babette looked at the man's flushed face again and frowned. In his feverish countenance she had not recognised the young man who had once visited her home—and to whom her father had intended she be betrothed. His hair was damp and straggling, his chin unshaven and there was a scar on his left cheek. He looked much older than the man she remembered, yet he might be even more attractive if he were well. It was the heat of the fever that had given him such a high colour and his unkempt appearance that had deceived her eyes into thinking him a stranger.

'You know of Drew?'

'He came to the castle once when we were younger, do you recall? It was the year after Mama died and before you left.'

'Yes, I remember, but I did not think you would, for you hardly spoke to him. He and I were out hunting most of the time and you were in mourning, shut away with your sewing most of the day.'

Babette acknowledged it was true, yet she had noticed their handsome guest and he had made her heart leap when he smiled at her once. Apart from that he had scarcely noticed her so it had come as a shock to her when Lord Harvey told her that he intended to seek a betrothal between them. She was not certain what would have happened had her father lived. He had told her that Drew's father was a great friend of his and the betrothal had been spoken of many years ago when she was born.

'Lady Melbourne and your mama put their heads together and planned that you two should marry, but nothing was promised. I have been lax in not arranging something before, Babette, but with your mama's loss—and then your brother...' Lord Harvey had sighed deeply. 'If the young man is in agreement, I see no reason why you should not be betrothed almost at once and wed at Christ's Mass.'

Unhappily, her father had taken ill and died long before anything was settled. Left alone at the castle until the King appointed a custodian, she had wept and waited, but Drew had not come to claim her. He did not even write to her, and Babette accepted that he did not wish to wed her. However, in her mind she had continued to think of him as the man she might have wed had her father lived long enough to arrange it—which was, of course, ridiculous.

Her patient had ceased to cry out in pain. The cooling water and the herbal mixture she had applied to his wound was easing the pain, though his fever continued to run high.

'Beth…thank you, sweetheart,' he murmured, a smile touching his lips. 'I love you…'

Babette's heart caught as she heard the words plainly. Now she understood why he had not come to claim her at the castle. He loved a girl called Beth, might even be betrothed to her. She felt a little pain about her heart, but it was soon gone for she had known that he did not wish to wed her and there was only a mild interest on her side. Had Drew wanted the match, he would have come to her after her father's death. It did not matter, though she must eventually marry. For though her brother needed her at the castle to comfort his wife while he was away fighting, his wife would in time wish to be the mistress of her own home. It had been a pleasant dream to be the wife of the handsome Cavalier, but one she must put away from her.

'He seems a little easier,' her brother said. 'You have brought us food—will you come again tomorrow?'

'I am not sure I can get away again tomorrow,' Babette said, knowing her aunt would think it odd if she wanted to go foraging again so soon. 'Perhaps I could slip down to the orchard…either this evening or early in the morning.'

'Come tonight. I shall be there when the church bells tolls the hour of nine. Did you come alone?'

'Jonas came with me. I told him to keep a watchful eye.'

'You can trust him,' John said, 'but do not tell him too much. Just say that I am alive and needed your help. The damned rebels would love to get their hands on Melbourne because he is important to the King's cause. I cannot tell you more, but believe me, they would pay a purse of gold for what you know, Babs.'

'I shall not betray you—either of you,' she promised and reached up to kiss his cheek. 'Be careful, John. Captain Colby's men are everywhere searching for supplies. If they should discover you…'

'I know. When Drew is able to ride we shall need a horse—but if the rebels have gone we shall come to the house and ask for help.'

'I am not sure that is wise,' Babette said. 'My uncle has chosen not to fight, but I believe his persuasion to be for Parliament, though he speaks only of wanting peace.'

'But you must return to the castle as soon as we leave. If you bring Jonas with you, you will be safe enough until we are with you. However, you must wait until Drew is better. It would not be safe for you to travel with just Jonas for company.'

'I brought only Jonas and one other with me when I came here,' she said. 'Tomas Brown went off to join the King's army. He told me what he meant to do and had my blessing—but Jonas is too old for campaigning, though he would fight if we were attacked at the castle, as all our people would.'

'He loved my father well.' John frowned. 'I was sad to learn of his death. I hope our quarrel did not hasten it?'

'Father died of a fever. He much regretted the breach and wished you home again.'

'I offered my sword to a foreign prince to support Alice, but when the King's nephew Prince Rupert decided to come and fight in England, I came with him.'

'And I am glad of it, for I have been anxious for you, John. Why did you never write?'

'I thought Father might forbid you my letters,' he said, a little sheepish. 'Forgive me. I dare say you were lonely—but you shall not be so, for Alice is already at the castle and waits for you impatiently.'

Babette nodded as she told her brother she longed to meet his wife and be of comfort to her. She would miss her aunt and cousin—her uncle, too, for he had been good to her in his way—but she would feel more comfortable in the castle now that Sir Matthew had invited a rebel to stay with them. She wished that she might have left immediately, but she knew she must wait until Drew was ready to travel; they needed her to bring them food and the healing cures her mother had taught her to make.

As she picked up her basket, an urgent whisper took her to the door. She opened it cautiously. Jonas stood there, looking anxious.

'Is something wrong?'

'I heard voices in the woods, mistress. We must go now—and tell your friends to be careful.'

'Yes, thank you,' she said. 'It is John come home to fight with Prince Rupert, Jonas—and his friend is wounded.'

'Praise the Lord my master's son is safe, but we must leave now. If those damned rebels see us loitering here, they will wonder. We should go now—and you must pick more herbs or your lady aunt will wonder what you did here all day. I have added some fungi I saw, but I know not what it is.'

'Thank you.' She turned to John. 'You heard Jonas—be prepared to defend yourself, but I shall try to draw them away if I can.'

'Take care yourself, Sister.'

Babette nodded. She hurried away from the hut, which was sheltered by thick bushes and thorns and not easy to find unless you knew where it was situated. She moved quickly until they had put some distance behind them, then began to fill her basket with herbs, berries and the leaves she wanted to make her fever mixture. Seeing the mushroom that Jonas had added she recognised it as poisonous and was about to remove it and throw it away when a party of horsemen entered the small clearing. She recognised them at once and her heart jumped with fright. Had Jonas not heard them in time they might have happened upon him and been suspicious of why he loitered in the woods.

'Mistress Harvey.' Captain Colby looked down at her, his forehead creased. 'What do you here?'

'I have been foraging,' Babette told him, lifting her chin. His eyes were suspicious as they centred on her, sending a thrill of fear through her—though her fear was for her brother and Drew rather than herself. 'I was not aware that I had to ask for your permission to look for herbs in these woods.'

Captain Colby dismounted, a flash of annoyance in his face. He looked at her in such a way that she felt he suspected her of an illicit meeting of some sort. Babette raised her head proudly, challenging him with her eyes.

'What have you in your basket?' he asked. He blocked her path as she tried to step away.

His eyes bored into her, making her heart jump. She felt his anger as cold as ice as he moved closer. She held the basket forward for him to see, and his mouth thinned.

'What is this?' he asked, pointing at the poisonous fungi with his finger. Now the suspicion was in his face. 'Do not say it was picked in error, for you would not be foraging at all if you were not aware of such dangers.' His gaze narrowed as she hesitated, seeming to become colder than ever. 'Were you hoping to feed it to me at supper somehow? You know that one small taste makes the stomach wrench with pain and enough of this is certain death to the eater.'

Babette looked at it as she sought for an answer, but Jonas came to her rescue. 'I picked it, thinking it good to eat. My mistress did not see me place it in the basket.'

'I was about to throw it away,' Babette said. 'Jonas picked the wrong fungi. I was busy picking herbs and did not realise.'

Captain Colby took the offending fungi in his gloved hand and threw it away, but the look he gave Babette told her that he doubted both her word and that of her servant. He truly suspected her of having picked it with the intent of doing him some harm. Her stomach clenched, for some men might have had her arrested and flogged—or imprisoned—on such a suspicion. She returned his cold look, tossing back her long hair, which glinted and took fire in a ray of sun reaching through the canopy.

'Take care when picking your mushrooms in future, mistress,' he said. 'A mistake like that can cost the life of a dear one—and if it was intended for an enemy it would be a bad mistake. My friends would have avenged me, and your aunt and her family might have been blamed.'

'It was meant for no one. Had you not come crashing through the trees it would already have been discarded. No harm was intended to anyone. Jonas made a simple mistake.'

'Have you finished your foraging?' he asked. 'We shall escort you home, mistress, for there are reports of dangerous men in this wood—and I should not wish you to fall foul of them, even if you do consider me your enemy.'

'We are of opposing beliefs, sir,' Babette replied with dignity. If he escorted her home, his men would not stumble on the hut that harboured her brother and Drew Melbourne. 'Yet

I do not think you precisely an enemy, for I believe you an honourable man.'

'Indeed?' His gaze became slightly puzzled, as if he was not sure whether to trust her. She prayed that he would not realise she wanted him gone from the woods. Had he suspected her reason for speaking him fair, he might have searched harder and found the hut that sheltered her brother. 'Then perhaps you will let me take you up on my horse. Your servant may take your basket back to the house.'

Babette felt trapped. If she refused him now, who knew what he might do? He already thought ill of her and was suspicious; if he decided to make a thorough search of the area he might stumble on the hut. She had no choice but to let him take her up, though the thought made her tremble inside. Hiding her trepidation, she turned to her servant.

'Take this back to the kitchen. Do not pick any more fungi,' she said. 'I must teach you what is good to eat and what is deadly.'

'Forgive me, mistress.'

Babette inclined her head. Hoping that her servant understood why she sounded harsh, she turned and waited for the Parliament captain to give her his hand to help her mount pillion behind him. Instead, he swept her up, his big hands one each side of her waist, lifting her to the front of the saddle with ease and mounting swiftly behind her so that his arms were about her when he caught the reins.

Her whole body trembled, unable to hide how much his nearness affected her. She was encased in a strong muscular embrace and could not have escaped had she wished. The masculine scent of him was as powerful as his physique, a mixture of horses, leather and fresh sweat and beneath it the smell of skin recently washed with a good soap. It was not the kind of soap her aunt might make at home, but had probably been made by a perfumery in France or perhaps some Eastern land, as it was infused with scents that were not familiar to her.

It was not the kind of scent often met with in the country, for the servants washed only when they changed their clothes and that might be any time between a week and two months. Aunt Minnie would not put up with slovenly dress in her servants and so those in the house were forced to wash both themselves and their clothes at least once a week, but many of the common folk seldom bathed. There were always the exceptions, of course, but many of them smelled unpleasant. Wealthy gentlemen often disguised their lack of cleanliness with strong perfumes imported from the East, but both Babette's family and her uncle's, were more conscious of the benefits of soap and water.

''Tis filth that breeds disease, if you ask me, and it be certain that it brings rats,' Aunt Minnie was fond of saying. 'I can't have folk in my house that carry lice in their hair or fleas on their body. If I find they have them, it's off with their things and into the lye bucket—and a scrubbing for them in the washtub.'

The cure seemed far the worst evil to her servants and most obliged their mistress by having a body wash once every week—and washing their hands and face each morning, and even before meals, if she were about to watch them.

This man had washed all over that day, for his scent was above all fresh. Babette found his smell comforting as well as pleasing. His hair was long, but it too had been freshly washed and was brushed back from his forehead and fell in soft waves to his shirt collar. Had it been cut short, she suspected it would curl tightly about his ears; the thought made her smile, for as a boy John had had ringlets, but when his hair was cut they were lost for ever and it now grew straight.

'You are thoughtful, mistress. Have I prevented a meeting with your lover?'

Was that why he'd insisted on escorting her home? Had he thought he was saving her from sinful behaviour here in the woods? She'd thought him more of a soldier than a religious zealot, but was he also a Puritan in his thoughts? Yet that did not accord with his scented soap and his fine linens—many of those who preached of godliness thought insufficiently of cleanliness in her experience.

'Why should I sneak away to the woods to meet a lover?' she asked with a flash of temper and perhaps unwisely. 'If I wished to court someone, I would ask him to come to the house.'

'I would have expected it of as proud a woman,' he agreed. 'Then what were you doing last night? You allowed me to think you were meeting a lover then.' She turned her head to look at him and saw the suspicion deepen in those deep-seeing eyes. 'Or are you a Royalist spy?'

Babette had to struggle against the shiver

of fear that threatened. He was so close to the truth. She managed to stop herself shuddering, sitting straight and stiff within the confines of his arms. His nearness made her feel weak and her throat tightened with an emotion she did not understand or wish to know.

'I do not know what I have done to make you think so ill of me, sir,' she said, meeting his eyes with her clear gaze. 'Someone I cared for came to the house to ask for medicine last night. I asked the symptoms and today I have been foraging so that I may make a cure for the fever that ails him—what is so terrible in that?'

'Are you then a witch?' he asked, but now the cold look had gone and a half-smile was on his lips. He was mocking her, but gently. Babette's heart beat faster, for his smile pleased her and made her wish he were not a Parliament man. 'Methinks I may have misjudged you last even, mistress.'

'You were quick to judge,' she said. 'There are in this world people—men—I care for, men who are not my lover yet who are held in high regard by me. Some might be relatives, others servants or merely friends; if any asked me for a cure I knew how to make I would make it—but I do not use spells nor do I ill wish any.'

'Yet he came to you in the dark of night.' Captain Colby looked thoughtful. 'I shall acquit you of wanting to poison me and mayhap I was wrong to think you had a lover—but you are hiding something from me, Mistress Babette. My instincts never lie. I must warn you to be careful. Please do not do anything foolish while my men and I stay at your uncle's house. Should I discover that you were harbouring an enemy I might be forced to take measures…and it would not go well with you or your family if a superior officer should discover you were a spy.'

Babette's heart caught with fear, not for herself, but for her brother and Drew. If these men should discover them she believed they would find themselves prisoners…perhaps worse. Could they be Royalist spies? John had seemed to hint that Drew was important to the cause. She must be very careful not to betray herself when John came that night.

'Now you will not speak to me,' Captain Colby said, a dangerous softness in his voice— dangerous, because it broke down her guard and almost made her forget he was her enemy.

Something in her responded to his stroking and she wished that she might confide in him. Why could he not have been a Royalist? Her throat tightened and she could not speak even if she wished. 'I did not wish to frighten you. I would not have harm come to you or your family, believe me. It was rather in the nature of a friendly warning.'

'Then I thank you,' she said, 'though I see no reason for your fears. I am merely a guest in my uncle's house. If my beliefs differ from his, still I would not do anything to harm him or his family. Nor would I deliberately harm you or your men, sir—even if we are enemies.'

'I hope you speak the truth for your own sake and mine,' he said, and for a moment his arms seemed to tighten about her. 'It would pain me if I had to punish you, Babs.'

How dared he call her by the name she thought reserved for her family? Her mood was instantly altered. She wanted to reproach him, but he seemed less angry and threatening and she dared not make him lose his temper again. She must ignore his familiarity while he was in a position of power—but if ever they should meet in different circumstances…

Contenting herself with thoughts of how she

would treat him with haughty disdain once the King had won the war, Babette managed to complete the ride back to her uncle's house without giving rein to her temper.

Once she was back at the house, Babette found herself busy cooking and baking. Now that they had so many guests there was three or four times the work. Aunt Minnie grumbled that the soldiers were eating her out of house and home, but Uncle Matthew reminded her that a troop of more than twenty men might have ridden in and taken all they had without any form of payment. Captain Colby had promised payment for what they took.

'I know your uncle is right,' Babette's aunt said when they were alone, 'but the work does not fall on him—and it will not be easy to replenish our stores. I may have to send to London for some supplies.'

'Yes, I dare say. We have used most of our spices, raisins and dates in the last batch of buns I made. You will need to buy more soon, Aunt.'

'I think I shall send to town for a length of cloth for Angelina and perhaps for myself. We could both do with a new gown for Sunday—

and perhaps you would care to buy something, too, Babette? We can have Mistress Hoskins from the village to help cut and sew it, though I like to finish my gowns myself.'

Babette hesitated. Had she not been told that John wished her to return to the castle she would have been glad of the chance to buy at least one length of wool to make herself a new gown for the winter months, which were not so very far ahead. However, it was unlikely that an order sent within the next few days would be filled and delivered before she was home again. Better to wait until she was at the castle. Perhaps Alice would care to order some cloth, too? Briefly, her thoughts dwelled on her sister-in-law—what was Alice like and would she welcome her husband's sister back to the castle?

'Thank you, dear Aunt,' she said, 'but I think I shall not order this time. Perhaps when the fair comes...'

She blushed a little as she turned away, not wanting her aunt to see her face. She felt guilty at hiding her secret from Aunt Minnie, because the lady had been kind and generous. Indeed, Babette would miss her when she left. However, she must rejoice at the news of her brother's return and her duty was to his wife. Alice was living in a strange house, carrying her first child and without friends. Babette knew how lonely it could be at the castle and thought that the sooner she was able to leave her uncle's house the better for Alice's sake. However, she could not leave until John was able to escort her. First he must get Drew on his feet again and then he must make certain that the Parliament soldiers had gone. Only then would he have time to fetch her.

After she had finished preparing supper, Babette began to brew an infusion of herbs and berry juice that she knew would help to ease the pain of Drew Melbourne's wound and to fight a fever. She ground her ingredients, poured on boiling water to release the flavours and healing properties, then strained the mixture through muslin, removing all the pulp and bits. When she had a clear yellowish-green mixture, she added a spoon of honey to sweeten it, tasted it, added more honey and then poured the finished preparation into a flask.

'You have spent a lot of time on your cure,' Aunt Minnie said. 'Who is it for?'

Babette hesitated. She thought that she might trust her aunt, but then the kitchen door opened and her uncle entered. She smiled and shook her head, slipping the small flask into the pocket of her gown. Aunt Minnie frowned, but remained silent, and Babette left the room. She went into the parlour and began to prepare the table for supper that night. The dark oak table looked best set with mats of woven straw, the knife to one side and the spoon to the other. In her uncle's house each member of the household was given both a knife and a spoon. Babette had heard that some people followed the French fashion and had introduced a two-pronged instrument into their households, which could be used to spear a piece of meat, but Uncle Matthew ate with his knife or spoon, using his fingers to secure any tasty morsel that could not be speared by the knife or scooped up in the spoon.

That night they were to have roasted capon. Babette's uncle liked the leg joint best and ate it with his fingers, disposing of the bones to the dogs he allowed to roam in and out of the house. They were hunting dogs, but also useful as guard dogs, and he liked to have one at his heels wherever he went, inside and out. Aunt

Minnie liked the breast meat, with the skin crisped and golden, while both Angelina and Babette enjoyed the sweeter meat on the wings. There was only one way to eat them and that was with the fingers, so they would need finger bowls set at intervals for each diner. She wondered whether Captain Colby would eat his chicken with the point of his knife or his fingers. He normally used the knife, spearing the meat and eating daintily until the last piece, which he ate with his fingers. She thought that his table manners were very good—the mark of a true gentleman. He had long narrow fingers that looked elegant when in repose, but which she knew to be extremely strong, having felt his grasp imprison her.

She must not think about such things! There were more important matters to concern her. She frowned as she remembered that her brother was to come to the house that night for the healing mixture she had brewed.

Her work in the parlour finished, Babette was just considering how soon after dinner she could slip outside to meet her brother when a slight noise behind her caught her off guard. She turned to see Captain Colby looking at her thoughtfully.

'Lost in thought, Mistress Babette?' he asked. 'I hope you are not planning to slip away to meet your lover tonight.'

Provoking creature! Did he imagine his mockery was amusing? The sparkle in his eyes was so attractive it made her angry. Did he think himself so charming that he would have her eating from his hand if he smiled at her? She would have liked to wipe that smug smile from his lips, but caution warned her to hold her tongue.

'You like to mock me, sir. I have no lover— and if I choose to visit a friend I think it no business of yours.'

'In times of war everything becomes the business of a careful commander,' he said, and his eyes took on the colour of wet slate.

'Excuse me, sir. I have work to do.'

For a moment she thought he would forbid her, and her heart raced, but then he stood aside.

'I must not keep you—but remember my warning.'

Babette drew her breath. She must be careful. She must not quarrel with him lest he have her confined to her room while he stayed in the house. Yet she could not allow him to intimidate her. John would be waiting for more food and the cure she'd made and she could not let him down. Inclining her head, she walked past Captain Colby and into the kitchen.

Dinner seemed to drag on for ever that evening. Babette ate her portion and rose to clear the dishes but her uncle motioned her to sit down and ordered the servants to clear the table.

'Remain with us in the parlour, Niece,' he said as his wife followed the servants from the room. 'Your aunt reminded me that you were born a lady and it was remiss of me to expect you to do chores more properly assigned to servants. Sit and listen. You may hear something of interest.'

Babette looked longingly at the parlour door, but she could not defy her uncle. To claim a headache two nights running would appear rude to their guest. She was forced to sit and listen to the two men talk of the war, of how it seemed to have reached a stalemate these past months.

'Neither side was truly prepared for it,' Captain Colby said. 'Tempers were raised and men threw down their ploughshares and took up swords, but most had no idea how to fight. What we need are trained soldiers and Cromwell is the only one of our commanders who sees how it must be done at the moment. His troop is the best equipped and the most disciplined of our troops.'

'Surely it would be better to make peace?' Sir Matthew said. 'Cromwell seeks to win a war with soldiers that are trained to fight— but it is still brother against brother and cousin against cousin. It would be better if the King could be brought to the table on some agreeable terms.'

'Perhaps,' Colby agreed and frowned. 'Yet there are too many hotheads that will not listen on both sides. They say Prince Rupert struts like a young cockerel and speaks of teaching the rabble to know their betters—such talk does not bode well for peace.'

'Will the King not listen to sense?'

'Why should he when he thinks he is in the right?' Colby asked. 'Had he been less stubborn, more inclined to listen to the views of those who understood the mood of the people, we should never have come to this situation.'

Babette sat, twisting her hands in her lap. She wished she had some sewing or perhaps a book of sonnets that might concentrate her thoughts. This talk of war and the allusions to the King were little short of treason to her mind. She felt like protesting, but bit her tongue, keeping the unruly thoughts from becoming speech. She would offend her uncle and their guest if she spoke what was in her mind—but oh, how angry she felt to hear such falsehoods. She was sure that the King was not half so stubborn nor yet as intransigent as he was made out—but why should these men try to dictate to him when he was King by divine right? They should know their duty to his Majesty…

'You are very thoughtful, mistress?'

Babette glanced up as Captain Colby looked at her, his fine brows arched mockingly.

'I was thinking that I promised my aunt I would help her prepare the oatmeal for breakfast,' she improvised. 'Forgive me, Uncle. I shall not be long—and when I return I shall bring my sewing.'

Before her uncle could refuse her, she rose and left quickly, though she saw Sir Matthew frown and knew he had wanted to keep her with him in the parlour. He had never required her company before, which meant he thought she should make the most of the time Captain Colby remained as his guest. Guessing that he was hoping their visitor would offer for her, she felt a surge of temper. How dared he interfere in her life? She would wish to marry one day, when John introduced her to a man she could like and admire, who would offer for her—but she would not be pushed into an arrangement that did not suit her. She would never, never wish to be the wife of a man like Captain Colby!

Escaping to the kitchen to find her aunt absent, she took oatmeal from the larder and put it to soak in a big earthenware bowl, then filled a linen bag with bread, cheese, the remains of a cheese and onion pasty and some cold cooked bacon. She added a flask of ale and the small bottle of fever mixture and fled before Aunt Minnie could return.

Glancing over her shoulder to make sure she was not observed, she had run swiftly to the appointed place. John was waiting at the gate that led to the orchard.

'Where have you been?' he hissed. 'I thought you weren't coming.'

'Be careful. Stay in the shadows,' Babette

warned. 'The soldiers' leader is suspicious. Sir Matthew kept me after dinner and I made a weak excuse to escape them. I must go back quickly or Captain Colby will think something is going on and he may have men watching for me.'

'Give me the food and medicine.'

Babette thrust it at him. 'Just a small dose every few hours—there is enough for two days. Do not use it all sooner or you might damage your friend further.'

'He is a little better since you tended him.'

'I am glad to hear it, but the fever may return.'

'Go back to the house. Send Jonas to the hut with food tomorrow, but do not risk it yourself. I will come for you when it is safe. Take care, Sister. I would not have you suffer for our sake.'

Babette thanked him and ran back to the house. Finding the kitchen still empty, she went through it and up the stairs to her room; she gathered her sewing, hurried back downstairs and re-entered the parlour, breathing deeply. Captain Colby looked at her hard, deep suspicion in his face. His look made her quail inwardly, but he made no comment. After a few moments, she thought she saw frustration enter his eyes. She thought it might be because her uncle had kept him talking longer and he had not been able to follow her and see what she did. Bending her head over the seat cover she was embroidering, she matched her threads and began to make the tiny neat stitches that made her work so attractive.

'You are industrious, mistress,' Captain Colby said, watching her intently. 'Do you enjoy your work?'

'Yes, sir. I like to be busy. I have been embroidering a set of cushions for the chairs in my aunt's bedroom. She finds my patterns pleasing and I wished to thank her for making me welcome here. I hope to have the set finished before I leave—' Breaking off abruptly, she cursed her slip.

'You are leaving us?' Sir Matthew frowned at her. 'Does your aunt know? This is the first I have heard of this.'

Babette berated herself silently for her mistake. She'd spoken without thinking, because she had not meant to mention her intention to leave until her brother came for her.

'I came only for a visit, Uncle,' she said,

a little lamely. 'I must return to my home in time.'

'Perhaps—' he frowned '—though my wife is your only blood relative, I think?'

'I have a brother, Uncle. If—if John returns home, he will expect to find me there.' She was feeling warm and uncomfortable, her skin flushing all over her body as she felt both Sir Matthew's and Captain Colby's eyes on her.

'Should Lord Harvey return you would have to go home,' Sir Matthew said, 'but until then, you must not think of leaving us—unless it was to a home of your own. It might be that I was able to arrange a respectable match for you.'

Babette kept her eyes downcast and held her silence. She did not wish to speak defiantly to her uncle unless she were forced—especially in front of Captain Colby. She wished Sir Matthew would not interfere in things that did not concern him. Her brother was the only one who could legally give her away, and she hoped she might persuade him to wait until she met someone she liked well enough to marry. Indeed, she believed he would be happy to have her remain single for the moment, at least until Alice had given birth to her child.

Time enough to think of her marriage then. Now that John was back in England he would bring friends and fellow officers to the castle when he visited Alice—and perhaps Babette would meet a man who could make her heart race and her body tingle in a way that gave her pleasure.

Meeting the cool gaze of the rebel captain, she was aware that her heart was racing wildly and a spasm of something half pleasure and half fear in her stomach made her feel quite weak. The way he looked at her…and the clean scent of his skin as they had ridden through the woods…

Realising where her thoughts were taking her, she brought them to an abrupt ending. Had Captain Colby been for the King he might have been just what she would like in a husband—but he was her enemy and she must never forget it.

Chapter Four

James Colby frowned as he looked out of the window of his bedchamber. It was plainly but adequately furnished and the bed was comfortable, but for the moment he was too restless to lie down. He wondered what it was about the Royalist girl with the bold eyes that had driven deep into his mind, reaching beneath the barrier he had built to keep out the pain.

He'd thought after his sweet Jane died he would be immune to a woman's wiles, but for some reason Mistress Babette had pricked him into constant awareness. She was the kind of woman that aroused a man's senses, but it was not entirely that… No, there was a spark of pride in her eyes and humour, a spirit that had not been crushed by her uncle's strict rules.

Despite himself, James liked the way she

had stood up to him in the woods, the way she matched him in thought and did not turn down her eyes as most women. There was no false modesty about her; she was prepared to speak out in defence of her beliefs, even though she knew his were opposite.

She was an industrious, thoughtful young woman, eager to work and help her aunt in the house. Her garden was much as Jane's garden had been when he'd first met and wooed her after his return from college. They had known each other as children, but it was only on his return from Cambridge that he'd known he wished to wed her. His delight and joy when she promised to be his wife and the promise of their first kiss had been all he'd needed. Jane had wanted to wait until her seventeenth birthday to wed and he had given way to her pleading for a little time, but a week before the wedding she'd taken sick of a fever and died. He'd been with her at the end, holding her hand, trying to give her his strength to pull her through the terrible sickness. As she faded, the life slowly ebbing from her, she'd wept and apologised for not marrying him three months earlier.

'Please do not,' he begged, emotion clogging

his throat as he looked down at her beloved
face. She was his dear friend, the companion of
his childhood years, now grown up and beautiful, and he had longed to make her happy.

Her passing had seemed to take all the joy
from his life. For weeks he hardly spoke to
another person. Life passed him by and he
had nothing to live for—and then someone
told him that the King had tried to arrest five
members of Parliament, all of them good honest men whose only crime was to speak out
against unfair laws. Having been the victim of
some of King Charles's taxes—and knowing
that a dear friend of his father had been un-
fairly convicted by the Star Chamber of being
a traitor and sent to the Tower to die, when
all he had done was to campaign for fairer
taxes—James was immediately on the side of
Parliament. How could the good citizens and
farmers of England accept the rule of a tyrant?

James Colby was not of the Puritan faith.
He believed in God and he disliked Catholic idolatry, but he loved beauty in all things.
A beautiful garden, a lovely woman, a pretty
gown trimmed with precious lace—or a valuable book bound in fine-tooled leather, silver
and gold, pearls and rare jewels, the scent of a

woman's hair… Mistress Babette smelled like honey and flowers.

The thought brought a smile to his lips and he chuckled as he thought of the way her eyes had taken fire when he'd accused her of being a witch. He had been unfair when he berated her for meeting a lover, for he would swear she was innocent, untouched. The smile left his eyes, because he was certain she was hiding something from him.

Why had she been out late at night? And then, in the woods, there had been something guilty about her. She was entitled to pick herbs and berries, but that mushroom…he knew it to be poisonous and so did she. So who had picked it? Her servant? Perhaps that bit was true, but surely he would have asked her…unless he was waiting for her while she spoke to someone else?

She'd told him that she was picking herbs to make a potion to help a friend, and he was inclined to believe her—but who was that friend? Why should she have looked guilty if she had no secret to protect?

Had she been meeting someone in the wood and if not a lover—who? Why had she been so anxious to leave the parlour earlier that evening? Afterwards, she'd returned with her sewing. He'd noticed mud on her shoe. She'd also spoken of leaving, which had been a surprise to her uncle. He would swear it had been a slip of the tongue—but why had it been in her mind?

Just what was Mistress Babs up to? Again, a smile touched his lips. She had not liked it when he called her thus. Was it a pet name? He felt a touch of jealousy as he wondered again if she had a sweetheart, yet why should he feel jealous?

His thoughts brought a frown to replace the smile. Had he truly considered making a girl he did not know his wife? He'd known almost immediately that Sir Matthew hoped for the match. He felt himself responsible for the girl in the absence of any other relative—and for some reason he feared that his son might take after the girl when he returned home from his college. He did not wish for a match between Babette and his son, so he hoped to marry her off to his second cousin before his son returned.

James had thought his cousin's hints and explanations clumsy, too eager, as if he wished to be rid of the girl—though she had a fair portion, if he had cared for such things. Sir Matthew had told him that her father had left her a small chest of silver and some valuable jewels, which were apparently lodged with the Jews of London for safe keeping until she married. Why did his cousin not think it a good match for his son? James would have thought it an excellent prospect for a young man about to enter the church—Mistress Babette was, in fact, above him in class and fortune.

Perhaps that was it, James reflected. His cousin lived an honest, hard-working life with few luxuries and little time for frivolity—and perhaps he sensed that such a life would not suit Mistress Babs for long.

She belonged in a beautiful house with graceful rooms filled with pretty things and should wear silks and velvets rather than the plain gowns that were all she needed for life in her uncle's house. James's house was filled with the beautiful things he'd planned to give to Jane—he had not been able to live there since she died.

His eyes darkened with pain. How could he even think of putting another woman in Jane's place? Yet in time he must marry and it was true that the Royalist girl had roused him from the depths of his grief. He did not love her, could never love anyone as he loved his sweet Jane…and yet…and yet… Riding with his arms about the girl and the scent of her in his nostrils, he'd felt a stirring in his loins. He had wanted to touch her, to caress her, bury his head in her hair and lay her down in a secluded glade within the wood to explore the delights of loving…

He had never made love to Jane in the physical way, never touched her pale flesh or kissed her deeply. How bitterly he had regretted that after her death, but in a strange way he had wanted to keep her on her pedestal to worship from afar. She was his gentle Jane, his love— and to despoil her with a man's greedy needs would somehow have been wrong. Of course when they married…

James frowned as he realised that he'd never felt tempted to take Jane down to the sweet earth and ravish her. How strange that he hadn't realised it before. He had wanted to protect and cherish her, but the powerful need Mistress Babs had aroused… No, he had not felt that with Jane.

He did not wish to marry the girl, even though he must wed one day to ensure an heir.

No, she was not fit to take Jane's place...and yet...and yet...he could not sleep for thinking of her.

If it were merely lust that she had aroused, then any woman would supply his needs...but despite his determination that she meant and could mean nothing to him, James knew that she had touched him in some way.

He wanted her as he never remembered wanting any other woman, her scent and presence in his arms arousing feelings that had lain dormant for too long. Yet it was not only that. Despite himself there was more.

No, he was a very wretch to think it. A surge of punishing grief pushed through him, and he shook his head. He would not betray Jane by thinking of Mistress Babs.

When he married it would be for comfort, nothing more....

Rising from her bed the next morning, Babette stretched and yawned. She'd had pleasant dreams, though she could not recall them, but they had left her feeling refreshed and happy. She poured water from her ewer into a bowl and washed her face and hands, then smoothed the washing cloth over her arms and breasts and down her body. Although she could not bathe as often here as at home, where the servants were at her beck and call, she liked to keep herself fresh and clean and her soap, which had been made in France and sent from London, was gentle on the skin and smelled of flowers.

When she had pulled on a clean gown of pale grey, thin woollen cloth, she went to the window and looked out into the back court-yard. Captain Colby was there, talking and laughing with his men, and she thought they must have been training or working for they all looked hot and, as she watched, several of them took a long drink from a jug of her aunt's good ale. Then Captain Colby pulled off his shirt and went to the pump, dipping his head under it. He shouted as the cold water cascaded over his head and shoulders, trickling down his back. Babette could not help but see that his skin had the soft golden colour that showed he sometimes worked with his shirt off, perhaps in his fields at home.

His shoulders were broad and he had strong muscles in his back and upper arms. It was hardly surprising that she could still feel the imprint of his hands where he had held her in the woods.

As he withdrew from the pump, he looked up at her window, his eyes meeting hers so intently that she drew back hurriedly. Her cheeks flushed as she realised he must think she was spying on him. Sensing that some of the other soldiers were about to follow his lead, she moved away from the window. She ought to have done so as soon as she saw what he intended, but she'd been fascinated by the strong tanned torso and the way the water had trickled from his hair down his back.

He was a handsome man and there was something very attractive about him, a masculine presence that made her feel as if she would like to be taken in his arms and held there safely. Babette admitted that she felt drawn to him against her will, because his smile was so charming that she sometimes forgot that he was her enemy—but she must not forget, because her brother's and Drew's life might depend upon her keeping up her guard. The rebel captain was a clever man and, if she allowed him to, he might discover her secret.

Babette finished her *toilette* and then left her room. When she reached the kitchen she found her uncle seated at the table drinking ale. It was their habit to eat in the kitchen at breakfast, for it saved the trouble of laying the table in the parlour. Babette went to the pantry and brought out the salted bacon, beginning to cut several thick slices. She fried them with slices of bread and brought them back to the table just as Captain Colby entered. He had put his shirt on again, but it clung wetly to his body and his hair was slicked back from his face and beginning to curl above his ears.

'Will you have porridge, sir?' she asked. 'Or fried bacon and bread?'

'Have you no mushrooms to offer me?' he asked and smiled at her.

'You need to be out early to gather them for everyone likes a tasty mushroom,' Aunt Minnie said, not understanding that it was a joke between them. 'I'm sure had my niece known you were partial to them, Captain, she would have risen early to pick them for you.'

'Thank you, ma'am, 'twas but an idle jest,' he said. 'I will have porridge—and some bread and a little of that excellent honey, thank you, mistress.'

'I shall pick some mushrooms for you to-morrow,' Babette promised.

'I fear I shall not be here to eat them,' he said. 'We shall be leaving you at first light tomorrow. I should be able to visit all the farms in the district your uncle thinks may have surplus to sell by this afternoon and then we shall avail ourselves of one more night of your hospitality, but we shall be long gone by the time you rise, mistress.'

He was going the next day. Relief rushed through her, but then she felt a tinge of regret. Once they parted she would never see him again—and why would she wish to? Instinctively, she raised her head, as if to protect herself from her own thoughts. He was her enemy, and she must forget they had ever met.

'Oh, must you leave?' Sir Matthew asked. 'I had thought you might make this your base and go further afield to find your supplies.'

'I am almost tempted,' Captain Colby said, 'but I fear I must press on. I am expected back within a certain time and must gather as much as I can. If I fail, others will be sent to use more forceful methods.'

'Then I shall come with you and lend my authority to you. We must see you have what you need before you leave.'

'Horses are my most pressing need,' Captain Colby said. 'You have a fine mare in your stables…'

'She is mine,' Babette said. 'She is my friend and I need her. She would not carry one of your men into battle. She is a lady's mount.'

His eyes met hers, and for a moment she thought he was about to overrule her wishes, but then he said, 'Unfortunately, that is true, mistress, as I was about to tell your uncle. Had she been up to my weight I would have given a fair price for her.'

'No money could buy my Darling,' Babette said. 'She is devoted to me and I to her.'

'I would not take her from you, Mistress Babette, but others might not be so nice. You must be careful not to ride out alone, for I think the times are difficult and you might lose both her and…' He frowned and shook his head.

Babette realised that he was hinting that she might lose her virtue and her cheeks burned. He was right, of course, for not every man she met would be as scrupulous as he and had she met a certain type of man in the wood… She shook her head because it was not a pleasant thought. She had always thought herself safe in her uncle's woods, but now there were too many strangers and it was no longer the case that she would be treated with respect because of who she was.

Babette put a plate of porridge and some fresh bread in front of him. He touched her hand and, when she looked down at him, said, 'I would speak with you later, mistress.'

'As you wish, sir,' she said, making a mental note to avoid him if she could. It would be much better for her if he left with her uncle and never returned.

After the men had eaten and left, Babette had helped her aunt to tidy the house and then gone out into the gardens. She tended the flowers and took a honeycomb from the hives, always careful to leave enough for the bees themselves.

'Thank you kindly, dear friends,' she said after she had filled her basin. 'May the sun shine and the flowers bloom for you.'

Babette had learned her craft from an old beekeeper, who had warned her that she must always thank the bees and wish them well, lest they be offended and leave the hive.

'Bees be very touchy folk, Mistress Babette. They gives generously, but expects respect.'

Despite herself, Babette found her thoughts

returning again and again to the rebel captain. Why did he wish to speak to her later? What could he have to say that was so important he had warned her of his intention?

Did he suspect that she had been tending a Royalist fugitive? Why was Drew Melbourne so important that John feared the rebel soldiers were searching for them?

A little shiver went through her as she wondered if he were a spy for the King, but then she thrust the idea from her mind. She must pretend to know nothing of them, for if one slip of hers betrayed them she would not forgive herself.

She spent the rest of the day baking, sorting linen and polishing. Every so often she looked out of the window, wishing that she dared slip away to the woods to enquire how her brother and Drew were managing, but John had told her to wait for him. She did not want to lead soldiers to their hiding place and forced herself to wait for the night in patience.

John would come for food and she would tell him the good news—the rebels were to move on and he would be able to bring Drew to the house. Her aunt would welcome them and give them food to see them on their way. If they travelled on horseback, as she thought they must, her trunk would have to be sent on to the castle by wagon. However, she would pack a few things so that she would be ready to leave when John came.

It was almost dusk when Babette saw the men returning. For a moment she could not make out what was happening, for they had brought three horses, two cows and a calf with them, besides some sacks of grain—but something was not as it should be. There was an air of apprehension about them, something that made her tingle at the nape of her neck. She was about to go out to investigate when her uncle came hurrying into the kitchen.

'Captain Colby has been wounded,' he said. 'I have sent someone for the doctor, but he is bleeding heavily. If his wound is not bound, I fear he may die before help can each him.'

Aunt Minnie gave a little scream. 'Lord have mercy,' she cried. 'Who would do such a thing?'

'We did not see, for we were fired on in the woods as we returned home. The first shot missed, but Colby went after whoever had fired, and another shot took him down. It was an attempt at cold, deliberate murder.'

Babette felt icy all over. Had John shot the rebel captain? Somehow she had not thought her brother a man to shoot another in ambush, to kill in cold blood. It would indeed be murder, and the idea that it could have been John made her shiver.

Her aunt seemed turned to stone, standing indecisively, a look of panic in her eyes. Babette cleared the table as the men brought the captain into the kitchen. He was unconscious, his face deathly pale, and she could see that he had lost a lot of blood.

'Lay him here,' she said in a tone of command. 'Aunt Minnie, a bowl of water as cold as you can get it, please, and some linen. I need a clean cloth to bathe him with and then lengths of it to bind him.'

'Yes, Babs,' her aunt said meekly. She had never hidden the fact that the sight of blood made her faint and turned her head as she offered the bowl. 'Angelina, go up to your room, please.'

'No, I shall stay and help Babs,' her cousin said. 'Give me the bowl, Mother. You go up and prepare the bed for him.'

Suddenly their roles had been reversed, for her cousin's tone was decisive and strong. Aunt Minnie, who looked on the verge of fainting, went without another word, and Angelina took her place. She held the bowl steadily and when the water was thick with blood she changed it without being asked.

Babette saw that the ball had penetrated only the first layer of flesh on Captain Colby's shoulder. She could see it protruding through his skin and decided that it would be better to cut it out than wait for the doctor. Instructing her cousin to light a candle, she held one of the sharp butchery knives to the flame for long enough to purify it and then plunged it into cold water. Inserting the pointed tip into the flesh, she made one clean cut, thrust the knife under the lead ball and flipped it out. It shot out and bounced on the table before running off the edge. Captain Colby screamed, opened his eyes, swore and tried to sit up.

'Forgive me,' Babette said. 'The ball is out and you will heal better with a clean wound.'

'Witch,' he muttered and fell back into a swoon.

Babette fetched a pot of healing balm from the medicine cupboard where her aunt kept her cures. It was some that Babette had made herself a couple of days earlier for Drew Melbourne in case he needed more. She applied a good scoop on to a pad of clean linen, pressed it to the wound and then asked her uncle to hold him up while she bound linen tightly over his chest and shoulder to hold it tight.

'You have a fine skill at nursing,' her uncle said, looking at her oddly. 'Who taught you—and why did Captain Colby call you a witch?'

'My mother taught me how to care for the sick. She nursed any who were ill at the castle—and it was in nursing a beggar who came to our door that she took a fever and died. Captain Colby was merely jesting, Uncle. He meant nothing by it.'

'Such jests are dangerous, Babette,' Sir Matthew said and looked at her coldly. 'I know you are innocent, but few young women could deal as skilfully with a man's injury—and folk are oft superstitious. It will go no further than this room, but should such rumours start you would not be safe here.'

Babette looked at him in shock and dismay. Why, he almost believed it himself! Yes, he did believe it. There was a wariness about him that she had never seen before and she knew he was suspicious of her art in healing—yet the salves were simple such as any woman with a little knowledge of herbs might make and she had used no incantations to make it.

Feeling slightly hurt that her uncle should even doubt her for a moment and puzzled that a man she had respected and thought intelligent should give way to foolish superstition over a jest, she realised that it would be as well if she were to leave his house soon.

Yet even as she longed to leave this house, which had seemed a place of peace and sanctuary until now, she knew she could not. Captain Colby would have died before the doctor could reach him. Her aunt was not good at nursing, though she did her best when one of the household was sick—and she would not permit Angelina to care for a man who was not a relative. Babette could not leave this house until he was strong and well again.

Somehow she would have to get a message to her brother and tell him that the rebel captain would not be leaving just yet.

In the morning, Sir Matthew told her that Captain Colby's second-in-command had decided to split their forces.

'Fourteen of the men will take the livestock and supplies they have bought and go on to the appointed meeting. Five will remain here to guard and escort their leader when he recovers—or carry news of his death if the worst happens.'

'He will not die,' Babette said more fiercely than she intended, for her uncle seemed to accept the inevitability of death too easily. Had it been left to him he would have prayed for his cousin and done no more.

The doctor had visited, praised Babette's work, given her a recipe for fever, which she already knew, and left, saying that she could do as much for her patient as he, and to send for him only if the arm became infected and needed amputation.

Babette had smiled and thanked him, relieved that he at least had not questioned her skills, nor thought of her as a witch. She had noticed one or two of her uncle's servants looking at her oddly, as he had a few times, though he continued to be polite and courteous to her when they met. Yet she had the feeling that he was uncomfortable with her in his house. He had become reserved, distant, and once she thought she saw fear in his eyes. Did he think that she might ill wish him?

Babette had visited Captain Colby three times in the night. For the first half of it he was burning up, tossing and turning, but at three in the morning he was cooler and no longer sweating. When she went in to see him at six that morning he opened his eyes and frowned at her.

'What are you doing here, Mistress Babs?'

'You were wounded badly, sir. I have been nursing you. Do you not remember? I had to cut out the ball. You screamed, opened your eyes and called me a witch.'

'Did I?' He smiled oddly. 'It must have hurt like hell to bring me out of that faint. Forgive me, mistress. I did not mean to insult you— and I do thank you sincerely for your help. I have been wounded before and lain in agony for days before a surgeon cut out the ball and that led to days and weeks of fever. It would appear that your treatment has saved me a deal of pain and sickness.'

'My uncle thinks me a witch because of it,' Babette said. 'I think he is a little afraid of me, though I have given him no cause.'

'If I have caused you harm through a foolish jest...' His forehead creased. 'It was not intended to be taken seriously, merely a teasing thing between us... Forgive me. I shall speak to him as soon as I get up.'

'You will not leave your bed today, sir. You lost a deal of blood before they got you home. Had I not acted as I did I think...'

'You think they would have let me die before the physician came?' He nodded. 'Not every woman has your skills or your cool head, mistress. I thank my good fortune that you were here—and perhaps one day I may repay you for your care of me.'

'If you can convince my uncle that I am not a witch and it was merely a jest, it will be enough,' Babette replied with a smile. 'I shall go now and fetch you some gruel...but I will bring you brandywine, too. My uncle keeps a small flask for such a purpose as this.'

Smiling at him, she left the room and went down to the kitchen, where her uncle and the servants had met her with strange looks. Somehow his fear of her had communicated itself to those who served him. How could he think that she was truly a witch—that she would harm the family who had shown her kindness and given her a home?

She hoped fervently that Captain Colby would soon be able to continue his journey so that she might return to the castle.

Chapter Five

As soon as she could get away, Babs took some food from the pantry and made her escape. She went alone and ran all the way to the hut where her brother and Drew Melbourne had taken shelter, her pulse racing. Would they still be here?

The hut looked deserted, but as she approached, a voice called to her from the bushes and she spun round, looking for whence it had come. The thorn bush rustled, and then her brother emerged, looking harassed.

'Soldiers were searching here yesterday and this morning,' he said. 'I dare not leave Drew alone, though he is better than he was. Has your rebel troop gone?'

'Some of them,' Babette said. 'Captain Colby was wounded yesterday evening as they passed through the woods. Most of his men took the goods they had purchased and went on to their headquarters, as arranged, but he is lying in bed at my uncle's house and five of his men remain to guard him.'

'Perhaps it was they who were searching,' John said and frowned. 'Who attacked him? Is there a Royalist force nearby? Could you get a message to them?'

'My uncle said nothing of a Royalist force,' Babette said and frowned. 'He called the attack on Captain Colby a cowardly ambush from the trees—the man did not face them, but hid and took a shot without revealing himself.'

'That is odd,' John said. 'It is not our way. We fight with fairness and honour. If a troop of his Majesty's men were in the woods, they would have fallen on the enemy and killed as many as they could, but to ambush one man from hiding—that smacks of cowardice and 'tis murder, not war.'

'It was not you?'

'What kind of a man do you think I am?' John looked offended, and his sister was quick to apologise.

'I did not truly think it, but I knew you were here and…' She frowned and shook her head.

'It would seem Captain Colby has an enemy. Perhaps a man with whom he has quarrelled.'

'It seems likely,' John said. 'With Drew still unable to travel I would not have risked it, especially when there were more than twenty of them. I saw them pass by, but Captain Colby was not harmed then.'

'How strange.' Babette was thoughtful as she went into the hut. She saw that Drew Melbourne was sitting in a raised position and fully conscious. He greeted her politely and thanked her for what she had done while he lay unconscious.

'John tells me I may owe my life to you, Mistress Harvey.'

'I did very little,' she said. 'I see you no longer need my fever mixture—but may I dress your arm for you again?'

'Thank you, if you will.'

He tried to rise, but she begged him to stay where he was and knelt beside him, binding him swiftly with clean linen and more of her healing salve.

'That feels much easier,' he said. 'I am in your debt, mistress. I must think of a way to thank you.'

'I need nothing but news of your recovery,'

she said and rose. 'I must go at once, for my uncle is suspicious and I would not bring danger to you. Jonas will come to tell you when the way is clear for you to come to the house.'

'We have decided not to ask my uncle for help,' John said. 'I found a man of Royalist persuasion who offered to help us and purchased a horse from him. We shall leave as soon as Drew can ride.'

'But you wanted me to return to the castle?'

'I shall send the coach to fetch you once I am home,' he said. 'My uncle might betray us if he knew we had been hiding in the woods. Say nothing to arouse his suspicions further, Babs—and wait for me to send for you.'

'Yes, if you wish. Excuse me, I must go.'

Leaving him, she walked swiftly through the woods and then ran through her uncle's fields and the orchard, noticing that there were more plums ready to be picked. Shaking a tree, she caught some in her apron and filled her basket. It would serve as an excuse if she were questioned when she returned home.

She wished that she might have gone home at once with her brother, for she no longer felt welcome in her uncle's house.

* * *

'Are you healing well, sir?' Sir Matthew said on entering the bedchamber where his cousin lay propped against a pile of feather pillows. 'My niece has made you comfortable?'

'Perfectly,' James said and looked at him hard. 'She is a good woman and skilled in simple healing ways. You must not misjudge her or take my jest seriously, sir. I but called her a witch in fun. I do not think it, believe me. She is honest and innocent.'

'So every man may think when bewitched,' Sir Matthew said and shook his head gravely. 'I did you a disservice, Cousin, when I suggested that you might wed her. 'Tis the reason I did not wish for a match between her and my son—her mother was a witch and, though I had seen no sign of it before, I fear she has taken after her.'

James was shocked, for he saw that his cousin was serious. 'No, how can you think it, sir? The girl is innocent and her healing is only meant to help, not harm.'

'Aye, when she chooses. But witches may change and bring about fearful things when they are angered. Her mother ill wished a man and he died. I know it for a fact, for I witnessed it myself. I saw his face after she lay her spell upon him and I saw him wither and die over the next few months…he was naught but skin and bone at the end. And Lady Harvey ill wished him because he dared to lay his hands on her daughter. He swore to me that it was but an innocent kiss, but the witch though he meant to molest her child and so she put her curse upon him and he died.' Sir Matthew made the sign of the cross over his breast and muttered something inaudible.

James felt cold all over. He did not believe in such spells, but he knew that many did and the power of suggestion could corrupt a man's mind and twist it so that he believed—and perhaps in that way he might think himself to death.

He pushed himself into a sitting position against the pillows to give his speech more authority. 'I do not think Mistress Babs a witch and I would be grateful if you will not repeat such things to anyone. She is the woman I would wed and I do not wish her reputation to be mired by this nonsense.'

'Think it nonsense if you choose,' Sir Matthew said, 'but when you leave, take her with you if you will have her—for I shall not suffer her here a day more than I need. She is my wife's niece and I do not wish her harm, but I cannot trust her.'

So saying he went from the room, leaving James to frown and worry at the foolishness and wicked harm some men did with their superstitions. His remark made when he was hardly in possession of his senses had only added to the suspicions already lodged in his cousin's mind. He had tolerated the girl here, but the old story lingered in his mind to haunt him. Sir Matthew had been determined his son should not fall for Mistress Babs's charms and now James knew why.

The man was a superstitious fool and there was no way James could leave Babs here at the mercy of a man like that. If anything should happen—the cows go sick or a man take a sudden illness—they might blame her and... A shudder went through him, for he knew what might happen to an innocent girl if such a rumour took hold. And all because he had laughed and called her a witch, because her smile made his heart leap.

When he left she must go with him. If she wished he would take her to her home, though if he had his way he would carry her off to his

own house and keep her safe, away from superstitious minds and evil tongues.

Babette entered the kitchen with her plums,
placing them in a bowl close to the sink in
order to wash them later. Her aunt looked at
her oddly, her normal friendly smile missing
as she asked, 'Where have you been, Niece?'

'I went for a walk and then collected these
on my way home. I saw they were ripe for
picking and if we leave them they will not last
long. Would you like me to stew them for supper tonight or bottle them?'

'Leave them to me,' her aunt said and looked
uncomfortable. 'Your uncle says he will eat
nothing you have prepared. I am sorry, Babette—but he has told me to send you home
as soon as you can be ready.'

'I know that I am no longer welcome here,
Aunt,' Babette said, saddened by her uncle's
attitude. 'All I did was save the captain's life.
Had I left it to the physician he would have
died before he arrived because he was losing
too much blood.'

'I am grateful for what you did, as your
uncle should be—but he is a superstitious man.
He thinks…' She lowered her voice. 'He thinks

you use witchcraft in your healing. I tried to tell him you use only simple herbs, but he does not believe me. He has always said your mother was a witch and now—' Aunt Minnie stopped as Greta entered the kitchen and shook her head. 'Take a tray to Captain Colby, Babette. He was asking for you earlier.'

Babette picked up the tray of food and drink and carried it up the stairs to the captain's room. Her throat was tight with emotion and she felt like weeping. Aunt Minnie was her only relative other than her brother and cousin, and now her uncle had banned her from his house. She would have to return to the castle and she did not even know if she would be allowed to stay here until John sent for her. If not, she and Jonas would have to go alone.

She knocked at Captain Colby's door and was bid enter. Carrying her tray in, she set it down on a table and poured some ale into a cup, taking it to the bed. She set it down on the chest beside him and went back to fetch food, but he caught at her arm, turning her. The touch of his hand made her stomach clench, and she tried to pull away, but he would not release her yet.

'Will you not look at me, mistress?'

Babette glanced at him, blinking back the tears that stung behind her eyes. Before he came she had been happy here, but because of his foolish teasing her uncle now believed her a witch and she had lost her home. He had truly been her enemy, though perhaps not intentionally.

'Something has upset you,' he said, eyes narrowed as he looked at her. 'What has your uncle said to you?'

Her throat was tight as she said, 'I am no longer welcome here. He wants me gone as soon as…as soon as you are able to fend for yourself. Since you are so much better, he will probably bid me leave tomorrow.'

'If he does, I shall leave with you.' He swore angrily, saying as she flinched, 'Forgive me, but the stupidity of credulous men who harbour such foolish ideas makes me furious. You are not a witch, Mistress Babs. You have done no harm to any and a great deal of good to me. It was my stupid tongue…and yet it was the reason he sought to promote a match between us. He already suspected you and wanted to keep his son safe from your influence. I think he thought you might bewitch the boy when he came home from college.'

'I do not even care for my cousin…' Babette wiped a tear from her cheek, tossing her head defiantly. 'What have I done that he should think so ill of me? I have not flaunted myself, wearing only plain dresses and no jewellery— why should he think me so wicked? What have I done to deserve his distrust?'

'I think it was rather your mother he thought a witch…until my foolish jest and the way you saved my life by your quick thinking. I am at fault and so I shall make reparation. I shall leave tomorrow and take you with me. My men and I will escort you to within a safe distance of your home.'

Babette felt tears sting her eyes. Once her pride would have rejected his offer instantly, but now she knew that she needed his protection and she was grateful for his offer. Yet even as she looked at him, her thoughts were of his own needs.

'You must rest longer, sir. You lost much blood.'

'And would have lost more were it not for your quick action. I cannot lie here and see you mistreated.'

Her uncle might send her away, and alone the journey would be hard and dangerous. She must allow him to help her, though it went ill with her pride.

'You may not be fit enough to leave in the morning.'

'I shall be fit enough to ride,' he said and smiled. 'I have been worse, yet still managed to do my duty. Do not concern yourself for me, Mistress Babs. Had I not made a stupid remark in jest you would not have been turned from your home.'

He spoke but the plain truth, and she needed his help.

She nodded, turning away from him before the tears could shame her. Leaving his chamber, she ran up the stairs intending to wash her face in cool water before returning to the kitchen. As she reached the door to her room, Angelina came running to her in tears.

'You mustn't go,' she said. 'I was lonely and bored before you came—and I shall be again. Please, take me with you. I want to come and stay with you, Babs. I love you.'

'I wish that I might ask you to stay,' Babette said. 'With all my heart I wish you were my sister and not my cousin. Your father would not allow you to come with me, Angelina. He thinks I am… He thinks me a bad influence on you.'

'He is wrong. Mother was always telling me to be more like you and praising you, but now she seems almost afraid to speak your name within his hearing. What have you done that was so terrible?'

'I have done nothing save cut the ball from Captain Colby's shoulder and given him a fever mixture to make him well. Please do not believe ill of me, Angie—no matter what people say of me. I promise you that I mean neither you nor your family harm. I love you and my aunt…'

'But not my father?' Angelina raised her head. 'I do not love him, either. He is stern and cold and I want to laugh and run in the meadows with you—not sit here and read my Bible.'

'You must obey your father and mother,' Babette said. 'If there were some way that you could come to me, I should welcome you—but only if it is allowed.' She embraced her cousin impulsively and kissed her cheek. 'Do not weep, dearest. One day a man will come and you will fall in love and then you may escape.'

'I do not wish to marry a man of my father's choosing. I want to come and live with you.'

Her cousin was in tears and, in comforting her, Babette lost the desire to weep. At least her cousin did not believe ill of her—and her aunt was unhappy at the situation. She might not believe that Babette was a witch, but she had to obey her husband.

Sir Matthew considered himself to be a just and fair man; he led a clean life, worked hard and worshipped God and expected his household to do the same—and for some reason he believed that Babette was a witch and in league with the Devil. Such a man could not harbour a servant of Satan in his house, though he had tried not to let his feelings show…perhaps because he feared her anger.

'You'd better wash your face before your father sees you,' Babette said. 'Say nothing to Sir Matthew. Perhaps one day we may think of a way to bring you to me, but until then you must be meek and attend to what he tells you.'

'Yes, for otherwise he would lock me up and give me only bread and water to drive out the evil,' Angelina said. 'I shall smile and be as meek as always—but I'm angry at what he has done and as soon as I can I shall escape and come to you.'

Babette made no answer. Her cousin was talking wildly. She was too young to wed yet and her parents would not dream of letting her leave them until the right husband was found for her. Had Sir Matthew not taken his niece in dislike he might have allowed his daughter to visit her, but in the circumstances it was unlikely—nay, it was impossible.

As Angelina gave her a small secret smile and turned away, Babette went into her own room and began to pack. As she folded her clothes and put them into her trunk, she saw that some of her things had been disturbed. Someone had moved the book of recipes that her mother had given her—she suspected that it had been read in the hope of discovering that she was using some form of the black arts, perhaps. They would find nothing incriminating in her notes. Her mother had been a good woman, a woman who gave selflessly of her time and knowledge to help others and she'd taught Babette to be the same—but she was not and had never been a witch.

Why her uncle should think it she had no

idea, but it seemed fixed in his head and there
was nothing she could do to change it.

Captain Colby ventured down to the parlour that evening. He looked pale and Babette
guessed that he was in some pain, but he bore
himself well and gave no sign of it. Babette's
aunt had told her that her uncle wished her
to take her place at table and be waited on.
She was not to serve any of them with food
or to help in the preparation of their supper. It
was as if her touch might contaminate others.
While it hurt her, she sat proudly and let her
aunt wait on her.

'May I pass you some bread, Mistress
Babette?' Captain Colby asked and passed
the plate so that she could take a piece. She
thanked him and selected a chunk, taking care
not to touch the rest of the bread. 'Would you
like cheese? Perhaps I may cut it for you?'

Babette thanked him for the attention. Her
uncle had taken his bread first and she noticed that he turned the plate so that his wife
selected from the opposite side to the one Babette had taken hers from. Aunt Minnie was
pale and silent throughout the meal. Angelina

defiantly took bread from the side her cousin had touched, her eyes flashing with pride as she looked across the table.

'Will you have more ale, Cousin?' she asked and got up to serve Babette. Her father gave her a reproving look, but she tossed her head and filled her own cup before taking her seat. 'I think the apple pie will not taste as sweet this night, Babs. Mother's pastry is not as light as yours—and it is so stupid—'

'Be quiet, Daughter.'

Angelina glared at her father, but before she could speak Babette shook her head, reminding her. She subsided into sullen silence, making her father look at her reprovingly.

'I shall be leaving in the morning,' Captain Colby said. 'Mistress Babette has granted me the pleasure of escorting her to her home. I must thank you for your hospitality, sir—and you, Lady Graham. You have been most generous to my men and me.'

'We were glad to have you, sir.' Aunt Minnie looked close to tears and, after one glance in her niece's direction, kept her eyes on her plate. 'I shall miss…' Her words were lost in her emotion. She was speaking to Babette, but dared not say what was in her heart.

* * *

Babette rose when the meal was ended to help clear the table, but Aunt Minnie shook her head at her. Feeling close to tears, she turned away and went out into the hall, intending to return to her room before she gave way to a storm of weeping.

'Mistress Babette.' Captain Colby's voice stopped her as she would have gone up the stairs. She hesitated, and he took hold of her arm. 'Do not let him distress you. He is not worth weeping over.'

'I am not weeping,' she said, her head up, though the tears were burning behind her eyes. 'It is mere foolishness…and so unfair.'

'It is my fault,' he said. 'I brought out his worst fears.'

'Yes, it is,' she cried. 'Had you not come here it would not have happened. You are my enemy and you have ruined my life.'

Wrenching away from him, she won free and ran on up the stairs. When she reached her room she gave way to the storm of emotion that shook her, but later, when the tears were spent, she regretted what had been said. Captain Colby would be within his rights to abandon her to her fate—but she knew that he would not.

He was her enemy, but an honourable man.

Babette was up early the next morning. She ate before anyone was down and then went back to collect the small pack, which was all she could carry on her mare. The trunk she'd packed would go in the wagon with Jonas and be pulled by the old grey cob, as it had been on the way here.

She spoke to Jonas in the yard, telling him that her brother and his friend would make their own way to the castle and that he must take her trunk and she would see him there.

'But how will you fare alone, mistress? You cannot travel on horseback by yourself.'

'Captain Colby will see me safe to the village and from there I can reach the castle alone.'

Her groom frowned, clearly disturbed by the idea. 'I mislike it, mistress. He is an enemy.'

'Of the King, yes—but he is not truly my enemy, Jonas. I helped save his life and he is grateful. Besides, I am no longer welcome here. My uncle thinks…' She could not bear to say the word. 'He does not want me in his house.'

'I've heard what they say. You are no such thing, mistress. If your father were alive, he would challenge that devil to a duel...and run a sword through his evil heart.'

'You must not speak so of my uncle,' she remonstrated. 'He is foolish, perhaps, but not evil. He is a godly man and much respected.'

'I've seen the likes of him before,' Jonas muttered. 'I mind when you were a lass... Evil comes in many forms, mistress. Sometimes it wears a smiling face, sometimes a frown, but behind the mask is a black heart. Your uncle speaks of justice and fairness, but he beats a servant for speaking out of turn and makes them go to church whether they will or no—and if they refuse, he turns them off without a hope or reference. If that be justice, I be the king of angels.'

'Oh, Jonas...' Babette laughed '...I thank God to have such a good friend in you. Go to the kitchen and my aunt will give you food for the journey and I shall see you in a few days.'

She turned as Captain Colby came into the courtyard, leading her mare and his own horse. He walked up to her and smiled.

'Are you ready to leave, mistress?'

'I said goodbye to my cousin earlier and to my aunt. You must not think ill of her, sir. She had tears in her eyes—but she must obey her husband.'

'I know she has no choice,' he agreed. 'Come, Mistress Babette. I shall put you up on your horse and we'll leave at once. I shall be glad to shake the dust of this place from my feet. Your uncle was fair enough to me, but I am angry at the way he has treated you.'

'It hurt me at first,' she said, 'but since you offered me your protection I shall come to no harm. Thank you for your kindness, Captain Colby. I should have found it harder to reach my home with only Jonas as escort.'

'His wagon can trundle in our wake,' he said and smiled. Reaching her into his arms, he swung her up into the saddle and then gave her the reins. They were about to move off when a shout stopped them and Aunt Minnie came flying from the kitchen, a small parcel in her hands.

'I'm sorry you have to leave us, dearest Babs. I've loved having you here—take this. It was a gift from your mother to me, but I have never been able to use it for Matthew forbade it. You should have it—and try to forgive me, if you can.'

'I have nothing to forgive.' Babette pushed the soft parcel into her bundle and smiled down at her aunt. 'I am sorry to leave. If ever you are in trouble, come to me—or send Angelina, if I can be of help.'

'He would beat us both,' her aunt said and looked fearfully at the house over her shoulder. 'Go now. If he saw me talking to you, he would be angry. He will make us pray on our knees for forgiveness this night for harbouring a disciple of the devil.' She crossed herself. 'Forgive me…'

'Come, Mistress Babs,' Captain Colby called to her. 'We should leave now.'

Aunt Minnie stepped back, tears in her eyes. Captain Colby led off, Babette close behind and his men following. She was not tempted to look back and thus did not see her cousin's mutinous face at the window, nor could she know that her uncle had locked his daughter in her chamber for safety's sake, lest she be tempted to follow her cousin into the darkness of evil.

She had come here out of loneliness and her aunt and cousin had been a delight to her. But now she knew she could never return to this house. She was saddened, regretting that her uncle could no longer trust or tolerate her near his family. She must forget the comfort of the manor house and return to her home and the bitter cold that was ever present within its thick walls.

Babette could only be grateful that her brother had taken his wife to the castle, for at least she would have company. She had been happy living with her aunt and Angelina and she would miss them very much. She hoped that Alice would like her and they could be friends, for life at the castle would otherwise be lonely again.

Would her brother be angry with her for accepting the escort of a rebel captain? He'd bidden her stay at the manor house until he sent for her, but how could she when her uncle would not have her beneath his roof another day?

John might be annoyed and feel that she had betrayed her principles, but surely he would understand?

She almost wished that she had never come to her aunt's home in the first place, but then... she would never have met Captain Colby.

Realising where her thoughts were taking

her, Babette tried to control them. She could not be falling in love with a rebel captain. It would be so foolish, yet in her heart she knew it was exactly what was happening to her.

No, she would resist, for nothing could ever come of such foolish thoughts. They had opposing beliefs and this war had made it impossible for them to be friends.

Soon they would part and she might never see him again, but for the moment they had the journey and who knew what might happen before its end?

Chapter Six

They had been riding for some hours when Captain Colby called a halt. Babette was feeling tired, for she had slept little the night before and she was relieved when he came to help her down, lifting her in his strong arms and smiling up at her in a way that made her heart race. Looking down into his attractive face, she felt a melting sensation inside, but resisted. She must not like him too much. It would be foolish.

'You are weary,' he said in a gentle tone. 'I should have stopped sooner, but I wanted to reach a safe house by eventide, for the inns are seldom to be trusted in these times.'

The look in his face was concerned and it made her throat tighten with emotion. 'Only a little,' she replied, touched by his care for her.

The seeming tenderness in his voice made her throat tighten and she wanted to stay within that charmed circle for ever. But he recalled his thoughts and let her go. 'I think my aunt sent food for us in the saddle bags—just simple fare, some cold pie, cheese and bread.'

'Her pies were not as good as yours. She will miss you, I think.'

'And I shall miss her. I was happy to cook for her—but my uncle thought I might poison the food and would not eat anything I touched.'

'The man is a fool.' He frowned. 'I once suspected you...that mushroom, but I was wrong.'

'You were right to think it dangerous. Jonas picked it in error.'

'While he waited for you?' Captain Colby looked at her hard. 'Who were you tending in the woods? A wounded Royalist? No, do not answer. It does not matter. I acquit you of trying to harm me—or anyone else. No doubt you were there on an errand of mercy.'

'I fear this is but poor fare,' Babette said, ignoring his question as she took him a parcel bound in linen. 'Not what you are used to, I think.'

'I am a soldier and eat what comes my way, mistress. You shall eat well this night, I promise you,' he said. 'The house at which we shall stay belongs to friends of mine—a gentleman who knows how to treat a lady. I did not like to see you treated little better than a servant in that man's house. You are better away from there.'

'Please do not, sir. I would not have had my aunt wait on me—and I took pleasure in baking.'

'Any woman may do that—but you were not shown the respect you deserved.'

Babette flushed, for she knew his anger was for her uncle. He had been furious at the way she'd been treated, though he had contained his anger while he needed to stay beneath her uncle's roof.

She had thought at one time that he liked his cousin, but now she saw that he had been forced to politeness by the need to humour Sir Matthew so that he had access to the local farmers. Was he then ruthlessly devoted to his cause? He had used Sir Matthew to help him purchase the stores he needed for the rebel army, but he'd admitted that if his stratagem had not worked he or another would have come in force and taken what they wanted.

Were all men ruthless when it came to the

cause they served? Babette knew that his smile sent her heart on a dizzy spiral, but what kind of a man was he truly?

No, she must not question. Without his help she would have been forced to travel alone, with only Jonas for protection—and in times like these there was no telling what might have happened to her.

Once left to herself, Babette unpacked the food from the saddlebags, which was just bread, cheese and some cold pie left over from the previous night. She spread her cloak on the ground and a rug and then set out the food, inviting the men in Captain Colby's command to eat. They thanked her, treating her with the respect her rank deserved, which she knew was because of their leader's attentions to her. Everything he said or did showed him to be a true gentleman and his care for her was all that she could ask.

Babette acquitted him of fault in the matter of his dealings with his cousin. He had a job to do and he had done it fairly, treating others with respect. Yet someone hated him enough to want him dead—someone who shot from the safety of trees and did not show his face.

After the men had taken food and moved

away, Captain Colby sat down on the dry grass next to her and took bread and cheese himself. Babette watched him eat it and smiled. He had a good appetite, but he ate in a mannerly way, even when using his fingers.

'Do you have an enemy, Captain Colby?' she asked as he wiped his mouth on the linen napkin her aunt had sent with the food. 'Do you know who tried to kill you?'

'We are a country at war. Any number of men might have tried to kill me.'

'Yes, that is true—but surely a Royalist troop would have attacked all of you. It seems to me that someone who shoots but remains hidden and does not show his face is a murderer. You were his intended victim—not my uncle or any other of your men.'

'Yes, it would appear so.' He looked at her thoughtfully. 'You are intelligent, Mistress Babs. I had not truly considered it. I thought mayhap some Royalist fugitives might be hiding in the woods and sought to kill an enemy.'

'Why pick you out? It was foolhardy in the extreme for, had your men chosen to follow, the fugitives would surely have been caught and hanged. I think they would not risk it for the sake of killing one man—besides, it is not their way. Had it been Royalists in any number they would have attacked you and tried to take your stores—a fugitive by his very nature seeks to evade. No, I think whoever tried to kill you wanted you alone dead.'

Captain Colby was thoughtful for a moment and then he frowned. 'Yes, perhaps. I had not thought he would resort to such a sly trick... but perhaps...'

'So you do know who it might be?'

'There is a man I know to be jealous of me. I have been fortunate and earned praise from my superiors, while he was reprimanded—and he blames me for reporting what happened. He made a foolish mistake when we were attacking an enemy position and when I was asked for my report I told what I saw. Though I laid no blame on him, it was clear that he was in command, and the mistake that got men killed was his. Yet he thought I should have lied for him, because we were once close. He was Jane's brother.'

'Jane?' Babette saw the look of grief in his eyes and her heart caught. What could make him look like that—as if his heart had been torn from his body?

'Jane Melchet was the lady I was to marry,

but she passed away. We were childhood friends and sweethearts, and I loved her very much.'

'I am sorry for your loss, sir.'

Babette could not trust herself to say more, for she saw by the raw grief in his face that he still loved the girl he should have married. She wanted to ask the question, but could not—and then he looked at her and she saw the nerve flicking at his temple. He was in such grief that her heart went out to him. She longed to hold him and kiss away his pain, but knew that he would not want such sympathy from her. He was grateful to her for saving his life, but she was just a Royalist girl—an enemy.

'She died of a fever just a few days before her seventeenth birthday—the day we were to marry.'

'Oh, how tragic,' Babette said, touched deeply by his pain and the thought of a young woman on the verge of marriage struck down and taken by a fever. 'What a terrible waste of life—and how sad for you all.'

Her words sounded so trite and could never convey the feeling that took her by the throat and made her want to weep for the pity of a young life wasted and love lost.

He inclined his head, his manner distant, as if he were lost in the past. 'Yes, it was a waste of life. She was bright and pretty and gentle—and we were all unbearably sad. Her brother was my friend. At least I thought him so, but he seemed to change after she died. I do not know if he blamed me.'

'Surely he could not?'

Captain Colby shook his head. 'I do not see how he could, yet he changed. He certainly blamed me for speaking of what I saw that day when he led his men into a trap. I spoke only the truth, but it led to his disfavour.'

'Would he try to murder you for such a thing?'

He shrugged. 'I do not know. If not Melchet, I know not who it should be, for I did not think I had enemies—except for those who ride under the King's banner.'

He had risen to his feet, and Babette did the same, gathering up the remains of the food and the rug and cloak. It was time to ride on if they were to reach their appointed destination that night.

He had told her so much and yet so little. She was not sure whether she wished her question unasked. His answers had revealed much that she had not known…a secret hurt that hurt her, too, because she knew that he could never love her as he'd loved his sweet Jane.

How foolish of her to care! He was merely a man she'd met by chance who was escorting her to her village. Once there he would say farewell; she would ride on to the castle and she would never see him again.

It was what she knew must happen, what she expected and wanted—wasn't it? Surely she would not wish him to declare feelings for her—to be asked for in marriage.

And yet he had said it was in his mind that day when they quarrelled. Had he said it in temper or merely in jest—in the same way as he'd called her a witch? It did not matter. To imagine a future that held him was ridiculous, for it could never be. She must put such dreams from her mind. He had been kind and courteous when she needed comfort, but there was no more to it—and she would be foolish to hope for more. Yet, when he looked at her sometimes, when he touched her, lifted her down from her horse, something leapt to life within her and made her long for…something she did not understand, something wanton and forbidden.

Such immodest thoughts!

Babette tried to forget the things he'd said and the way he'd looked at her, the feel of his arms holding her safe, the gentle caress of his voice when he took her from her uncle's house. All these things meant nothing, were probably her imagining. He could not love her, because his heart was in Jane's grave—and even if he did, she could never marry him.

They were enemies. Her brother John was this man's enemy. If they met on the field of battle, they would try to kill one another—how could she even think of marriage?

It was ridiculous. She did not know where the thought had come from or why. His smile made her heart race, but that did not mean... And yet she knew that she had begun to feel so much more for this man than she ought.

No, she was being emotional and foolish. Just because her uncle had turned her out and this man had rescued her.

She would put all such nonsense from her mind.

Looking about her as they continued their journey, Babette thought it was odd or per- haps fortunate that they had not met with any Royalist soldiers. Although no large battles

had been fought of late, there were often skirmishes between local troops, and she knew
that the nearer they got to the castle, the more
likely it would be that they would run into a
troop of the King's men.

James glanced at the woman's face as she
rode. She was lovelier than he had thought at
the start; even when sad her face had something sweet and haunting about it. Her bold
eyes could flash with temper and when she
defied him he wanted to tame her. But most
of the time he wanted to kiss her, to take her
down with him to the dry earth and love her.

Had he believed in such things he would
truly have thought she had bewitched him.
The feelings he had for her were so different
to those he had held for Jane for such a long
time. Jane had been gentle and mild, a girl who
would always seek to please, full of doubts and
anxious to do what he wanted. Perhaps her
anxiety had contributed to her illness? Was
that why her brother hated him?

He and Herbert Melchet had been friends
from childhood, learning to ride their ponies at
the same time, fighting, playing, growing up in
the same woods that bordered their parents' es-

tates. Did Herbert think that he'd put pressure on Jane to make her agree to wed him? Could it possibly be he who had tried to kill him?

Mistress Babette thought he had an enemy and, when he considered, James could only agree. Someone had wanted him dead—but was it Jane's brother?

He dismissed it from his thoughts, looking about him as they rode. They had been fortunate not to come up against a Royalist troop. The closer they got to Babette's home and the Royalist stronghold, the more likely it became that they would meet an expeditionary force. He did not have enough men to fight so he would have to take avoiding measures. Much as that went against the grain, he would do it rather than risk Babette's life.

His brow creased as he thought of the future. When they got close enough to her home, he must say farewell to her—and that would not be easy. Somehow the barriers between them had crumbled since she saved him from being left to bleed, perhaps to death. He did not doubt that Lady Graham might have tried to patch him up, but it was Babette's skill that had undoubtedly saved him weeks of suffering. If the ball had been left in too long it might have led to putrid flesh and perhaps the loss of his arm. He had seen it often enough when a man had been neglected—or butchered by the surgeons with their infected knives that were used time and time again without cleansing.

He undoubtedly owed the fact that he was able to ride to Babette, even though his wound had begun to pain him. Frowning, he knew that he ought to have asked her to renew the bandage when they stopped. He would do so later, because it was becoming very painful and he did not wish to succumb to a fever now.

Yes, he would ask her to bind his wound again. The thought of her hands touching him made him breathe harder. He struggled to control the burning need that spread through him like wildfire. She was an innocent, and he could not despoil her—even though he wanted her more than he had ever wanted any other woman.

More than Jane? James faced the truth. He had never felt this way when he was with Jane. Yes, he loved her, but he had not felt this burning physical desire.

His thoughts were sombre. Was he betraying Jane in his thoughts? He must not! She was all he had loved and wanted—and yet a tiny corner of his mind was telling him that had they married she would not have welcomed James to her bed.

No! He was wicked to have such thoughts and must put them from his mind. The Royalist girl deserved his gratitude, but nothing more. He would forget her as soon as they were parted.

She had saved his life and he was grateful. He could not have done less than escort her home…but if that were all, why did he have this empty feeling inside at the thought of their parting?

The house they stayed at that night was a large, comfortable manor house. With long, gracious rooms panelled in oak and well furnished with carved stools, chairs, settles, court cupboards and stout tables with bulbous legs, it was an elegant home. Pictures and expensive ornate mirrors adorned the walls here and there—there were even some carpets on the floors.

In the castle the carpets were used to hang on the walls to keep out the chill off the thick stone, but here they added colour and brightness to the best parlour floor. Much of the silver that would normally have graced such a room had been put away or melted down for the cause, but there was plenty of burnished pewter, brass and ironwork. Also, some wonderful bowls fashioned of hard stone that Babette knew to be alabaster or perhaps jade and was a wonderful milky-white colour. Her father had one such precious bowl at home, which she knew had come from the Far East and had been brought back by some enterprising trader. During the reign of Elizabeth I the sea captains had become more and more daring, venturing to the trade routes of China, Arabia and the Indies, bringing back treasures that had seldom been seen in England, other than the few trinkets brought back by the conquering Crusaders. Now what had once been rare beyond price was becoming more often met with as the world opened up for the daring merchant-adventurers who risked their lives for spices, silks, gold, rich carpets and precious things from the East.

Sir Matthew's house contained none of these luxuries. He would have frowned on such ostentation, but Babette appreciated the beauty she saw around her—and the kindness of the host and hostess who welcomed her to their home for Captain Colby's sake.

'It is a privilege for us to have the daughter of Lord Harvey stay,' Sir Michael Hastings said, smiling at her after they had supped together. 'I knew your father well when we were young men—and I have met your brother. John is serving with his Majesty. He and Drew Melbourne are important courtiers and highly thought of by the King.'

'Thank you for your kind words,' Babette said and looked puzzled. She had not expected to hear kind things of her brother here. 'I knew my brother was serving his Majesty, but I did not know in what capacity...' She hesitated, then, 'But are you not for Parliament, sir?'

'I fight for neither side, but I am in touch both with the King and with Lord Manchester, who is fighting against his Majesty. We and others would bring about a truce if we can and see an end to this war.'

Babette looked at Captain Colby. He did not look shocked and she realised that he must have known his friend was neutral; he had chosen to fight against the injustice of the harsh laws that had been made, some said by the King's council rather than he himself, but retained his friendship for a man who seemed slightly more Royalist than rebel.

She caught a thoughtful look in Captain Colby's eyes and wondered at it until she recalled what she'd said. He must have heard from her uncle that her brother had disappeared and she had just admitted to knowing her brother was in the King's service.

Her cheeks warm, she turned away from the accusing look in his eyes and allowed her hostess to conduct her to her chamber. Lady Hastings was a plump, pretty lady of perhaps nine-and-twenty years. She liked to talk and chattered on about all manner of inconsequential things as she led the way.

Her gown was of the best silk and a pale blue in colour. It rustled and swayed as she walked, the full panniers holding out the wide skirts which swept the ground as she made her stately progress along the upper hall. Babette felt dowdy in her simple gown of grey and wished she had one of her own silk gowns to wear.

'This will be your room, Mistress Babette,' she said, stopping in front of a door. 'I hope you will be comfortable here.'

Babette looked about her. The bed was a

half-tester with carved oak posts hung with green-velvet curtains caught back with ropes of twisted gold thread. The coverlet was a patchwork of green, red, gold, cream and yellow, and the pillows were feather-filled and piled high, the sheets of the finest linen, to be seen where the coverlet had been turned back invitingly. At each side of the bed was a small side table upon which stood iron candelabra. There was a large cupboard with space underneath to store a trunk and shelves above to lay her gowns. Also a chair with legs that curved in an X-shape, a coffer on legs set with silver trinkets and an embroidered cloth, and at the end of the bed a long stool with a padded, embroidered seat in colours of rose and gold. This was luxury indeed, for her room at home was smaller, though as comfortable because she had her needlework stands, her lyre, harp and other personal belongings—things that she had not chosen to take with her to her uncle's house.

'This is beautiful,' she said with honesty. 'No one could fail to be comfortable here, ma'am.'

Lady Hastings looked pleased. 'It is our third-best guest chamber,' she admitted. 'Captain Colby is a good friend of our family and we could not do less for a lady he brings to visit us. The best guest chamber is reserved for his Majesty. It is the State Room and much grander, but I think less comfortable.'

'Has the King stayed here?'

'Oh, yes, many times in the past.' Lady Hastings frowned. 'You think it strange that we respect the King, yet welcome his enemies here? We have many friends, Mistress Babette. I should hate to quarrel with any of them and if the time comes when we must choose it will be very hard.'

'Yes…' Babette bit her lip. She had wondered at it, for though her uncle professed to be neutral he had made no secret that he was for the rebels when it came to it. In this house she sensed that the owners were truly neutral and wished only for a peaceful solution to the discord that was tearing the country apart. 'Captain Colby says he is for Parliament, but he is not like the men who rant and preach against all pleasure.'

'Puritans!' The lady curled her lip in disgust. 'If I thought that they would win the day, I should take up a sword and fight for the King myself. James is no Puritan, mistress. He is a generous, charming man who loves the finer things of life, as we do, and wants only to live in an England where all men have rights and none are unjustly punished. My uncle was condemned and tried by the Star Chamber, though all he did was complain about the tax of Ship Money and refuse to pay it. Because he urged others to do the same they arrested him and tried him—he was tortured to make him confess his treason to the Crown. When he would not break, they threw him in the Tower and he died there of a fever.'

'Oh, how cruel,' Babette cried, horrified. 'I did not know King Charles allowed such wickedness in his name.'

'Lord Hastings believes it is the Catholics in his council who do these things. He should renounce them and recall Parliament—and then there would be no need for this foolish war.'

'Yes, he should,' Babette said. 'I did not know what the Star Chamber did—and I think it should be disbanded. Such cruel ways are not fitting in this England. My father did not approve of the Pope or the Catholic faith—and I think you feel the same, ma'am?'

'No wonder James likes you,' Lady Hastings cried and kissed her cheek. 'You think as we

do, my dear. I am so glad to have met you—
and you must call me Suzette. We shall be
friends when you wed James, of course. He is
of the Protestant persuasion, as we are. I know
nothing is settled and forgive me if I speak out
of turn, but I saw the way he looked at you—
and I know you would not have consented to
his escort if there was nothing between you,
for it would not be proper.'

Babette turned away, her cheeks flaming.
Her hostess had spoken so openly and, of
course, what she said was true—it was most
improper for her to travel with only a male escort that was not family, unless there was an
understanding between them. Her eyes went
towards the open door and she saw Captain
Colby standing there. She knew at once that
he had heard his hostess, and her mouth quiv-
ered as she put a hand to her face. How embar-
rassing that he should have heard every word!

She hoped he would just walk away, pretend that he had not heard, but instead he came
into the room, smiling at her and then at Lady
Hastings.

'I am hoping that Mistress Babette will give
me her heart and her hand,' he said in a clear
firm voice. 'However, as you know, Suzette,

her brother is for his Majesty while I fight for the rebels…as he would name us. Not everyone is as tolerant as you and Michael. Our arrangement has to remain a secret until I can speak to Lord Harvey and that may be some time…perhaps not until the war ends. If I were to ask too soon, he might refuse us, for unfortunately we are as enemies.'

Lady Hastings made a distressed clucking sound in her throat and shook her head. 'How awkward for you both. I understand completely and shall keep your secret—but I can see that you care for each other and I shall pray that in time you may be together and happy.'

'I pray for such good fortune,' Captain Colby said. 'Forgive me for intruding on your privacy, ladies. I came only to say that Babette's trunk has caught up with us if there is anything she needs from it?'

'I thank you, no,' Babette said. 'All I need for the night is in my bundle. If you will make my servant comfortable for the night, ma'am, I shall be grateful.'

'Of course. He may sleep in the kitchens with the others,' the lady said, 'and I shall personally see to it that he has all he needs. I will leave you to settle in. James, have you all you require in your chamber?'

'Yes, thank you, Suzette,' he said and smiled at her, offering his arm.

Babette closed the door, watching as they walked away down the hall together. He turned his head to look at her, his eyes conveying some kind of message she did not quite understand. After closing the door, she considered what had happened and realised what his message must mean: he had been obliged to tell his hostess that there was an understanding between them to save her reputation. Naturally, it meant nothing and he wanted her to understand that it was simply an excuse to save her face.

How she wished that it were the truth!

She swallowed hard, knowing that she wished with all her heart that the situation were as he had described. To leave him when they reached her village and know they would not meet again was very hard.

Babette was conscious of an odd ache in her chest. The rebel captain had come to mean far more to her than was good for her.

James had gone to Babette's room in the hope of asking her to rebind his shoulder, but having overheard Lady Hastings he could do nothing but claim that he intended to wed Babette. By bringing her here he had exposed her to conjecture and a possible loss of reputation. She had travelled with him and his men all day with no female companion. In his haste to remove her from her uncle's house, he had not thought of what his friends might think. Now he knew that he had placed her in a difficult position. There was only one way to make amends—and that was to offer for her.

He could not approach her brother while they were at war, but if Lady Hastings believed they were to marry she would not think of Babette as wanton or careless of her reputation. So he had spoken out—and, strange as it was, in speaking of a marriage between them, James had seen that it would suit him very well.

Babette was beautiful, but she was also all that any reasonable man could require in a wife. She had skills that would benefit his household, knowledge of herbs and cures that were often needed in a large house where someone was always requiring some attention. Her pies and pastry were far better than her aunt's—and…at last he admitted what he had been fighting for days. He wanted her as a man wants a woman in his bed.

James had been celibate too long. He had not touched a woman since he had last kissed Jane. He had thought of going to the whores with his men on a couple of occasions, for like any other man he had needs, but something had held him back. Perhaps he feared to besmirch Jane's memory—or perhaps he was merely too fastidious.

Babette's smell was clean and fresh, a delicate perfume hanging about her that seemed to hint at roses and lavender without being overpowering. He had been tempted on several occasions by her—and he knew that there was fire in her. Besides, there were hidden depths in her—a mystery he wished to solve. He knew with his heart and soul that there was more to his feelings for her than his mind would allow.

His mind told him that he must continue to mourn Jane, but his heart and body cried out that he had grieved long enough—and that Babette was the woman who had healed him. She had brought him kicking and screaming back to life, though he'd clung to his grief—but she had made him aware how sweet life could be once more.

Why then should he look elsewhere for a wife? He must marry in time, for he did not wish to spend his life alone. He would always regret Jane's death, though a voice in his head told him that his gentle love would not have enjoyed the marriage bed…she was too ethereal, too good for this world. Perhaps that was why God had seen fit to take her?

Babette Harvey was all woman, passion and fire and voluptuous flesh. She was the kind of woman who could match him—who would give him children and warm his bed for years to come. It would be no sacrifice to wed her.

Besides, he hardly had a choice, for he was too much the gentleman to ruin her reputation and then ride away and leave her to face the consequences. No, he would offer her an honourable marriage. It was the best solution for them both.

After a night of lying restless in her bed for hours, Babette was brought a cup of ale, rolls and honey to her room just before it was light the next morning. The maid then went away, leaving her to break her fast and returning with a jug of warm water some minutes later.

'The rolls and honey were delicious, as was

the ale,' she said. 'You are spoiling me. I could have risen had you told me at what hour you break your fast here.'

'Captain Colby asked that you be woken and served early before the master and mistress generally rise,' the young servant said with a blush of pleasure. 'He wishes you to go down as soon as you are ready for he must continue his journey by first light.'

Babette hid her sigh of disappointment. She had hoped they might stay here a little longer, for she liked this house and the people who lived here. The sooner they left, the sooner she must part from her escort and that thought caused an ache in her breast.

However, she knew that Captain Colby was a busy man and she must not take up more of his time than she was forced to, because he had important work waiting. He would have to explain himself to his superiors, for they would wonder why he had gone out of his way to help an enemy. Yet he was risking more than just his reputation by bringing her home; he and his men could be set upon by a roving force of Royalist soldiers and might lose their lives because of her.

Sobered by this thought, she went down

as soon as she had put on her cloak. Captain Colby was in the hall saying goodbye to their host. He turned and looked at her with approval as she reached the bottom stair.

'Good morrow, mistress. You are in good time.'

'An example to us all,' her host said, smiling.

'Thank you for a kindly welcome, sir,' she said, addressing Lord Hastings. 'I slept most comfortably.' Not true, for her thoughts had disturbed her rest too often.

'My wife apologises for not being down to bid you farewell, but she does not rise for another hour or more.' He took the hand Babette offered and raised it his lips. 'I have enjoyed meeting you, though I could have wished for a longer stay—but perhaps James will bring you here again one day.'

'Perhaps...yes, I should like that very much,' Babette said with a faint flush. She could do no other though she was conscious of Captain Colby's eyes on her. She did not wish him to think she expected him to keep his word to ask for her. He was under no such obligation and had spoken only to save her face in front of Lady Hastings. 'May God keep you and your family, sir—and I pray for peace and a just settlement, as you do.'

With these words and more of their like they parted from their host and went outside. The horses were waiting. Babette walked to hers, then turned and gave her hand to Captain Colby. He smiled at her.

'Do not look so awkward. I said what I said last night because it was needful—but if you mislike it so much I can find an excuse to explain to my friends one day.'

'I do not understand…' Babette faltered. 'I did not think you meant…you spoke only to save my modesty, I think?'

'I spoke to save the reputation of a woman I greatly admire—a woman I should ask for if things were otherwise.' His eyes seemed to burn into her. 'You must know that I have come to care for and respect you. If I were free, I would court you, as your rank deserves, but the war has swept all chance of that away. I would have you as my wife with the permission of your brother, if I knew how that might be got. If you care to wait for the end of the war…'

Babette did not know how to answer him at once, for he had taken her breath away.

'You honour me, sir. I thank you for the compliment…but we hardly know one another. I would not have you feel obliged when there is no need.'

'I think I know you, Babs,' he said, his gaze narrowing. 'I wondered who you met that night and in the woods, but now I think I know. Your brother came to you for help in secret, I believe?'

She hesitated, then inclined her head. 'Yes, that is so, sir. He is, as you know, a Royalist, but I did nothing that would harm anyone. All I sought to do was help someone in trouble.'

'As you did me when I was wounded. I am aware that I owe you my life, Babs. Yet it is not for that reason that I offer you my hand. We may not know each other well, but I find myself attracted to you and I think we might deal well together. I do not speak only from obligation—though I would not have you suffer loss of reputation.'

'Lady Hastings will forget me. You may explain to her one day, if you wish.'

'You do not think we might suit?'

'Yes, I think perhaps we should,' she replied honestly, raising her eyes to his. Her heart raced and, for one moment, she was tempted to say that she would go away with him, forget her duty to her family, forget the war—but then reality took hold and she knew it was impossible. 'Yet at this time it would not be right or proper in me to marry a man who is the enemy of my family.'

'I am not your enemy,' he said softly, 'but I respect your feelings and I shall wait until the time is right to ask again.'

He would ask her again! For a moment she could not breathe.

Babette's throat tightened and she wished that she could throw caution to the winds, tell him that she liked him more than any man she had ever met and go with him. Yet if she did she might never see her brother again, for he would think that she had betrayed him and his cause. The pain about her heart was intense, but she turned her head aside so that Captain Colby should not see her pain and indecision.

He took hold of her, both hands about her waist, tossing her up on her horse's back and giving her the reins. She felt as if her body were on fire and wanted to cling to him, to let him kiss her until she forgot all else—but common sense made her hold back. She could not love an enemy.

Babette had to fight her tears as he walked away from her, but she raised her head and controlled her wilful need. She was the daughter and sister of a lord of the realm and both her father and brother had always been loyal to the King—as she must be. To marry a man who had taken up arms against his King would betray all she had been taught to believe in… and yet her heart cried out that this man was the one man in all the world who could make her happy.

Captain Colby had given the order to move off. Babette gripped her reins and followed, her eyes blinded by the tears she could not quite control. She was denying her heart to do what she believed was right—and she must not weaken, even if her heart felt as if it would break in two.

They travelled all that day, stopping only once to eat food their host had sent with them from his kitchens. Captain Colby was courteous, polite, but a little reserved. Babette suspected that she might have hurt his pride by dismissing his offer out of hand.

She prayed that she had not hurt him, because she cared for his good opinion and liked him well. She dare not attribute a deeper meaning to her feelings towards him, for if she once admitted her love she would lose the strength to resist—and resist she must.

It was approaching dusk when they saw the castle outlined against the darkening sky. Captain Colby halted his men a short distance from the village. He turned his horse and came back to her, his eyes intent on her face as he said, 'I shall ride the last mile alone with you, mistress. My men will stay here, for if we approached the castle it might be mistaken as a hostile attack.'

'I would not have harm come to you or your men,' she said, blinking back the betraying tears. 'I am close to home and none would harm me here. I am well known and liked, I think. Leave me now, sir, and go on your way. I have taken enough of your time.'

'I shall ride with you until you are within sight of the walls,' he insisted. 'My men will wait here until I return—for an hour at least. If I should not return, they would then go on without me.'

Babette wanted to deny him, but his face was set and she knew he would not desert her.

He would insist on accompanying her to her home at the risk of his own safety. She thanked him, turning to lead the way. He brought his horse to walk by her side and, risking a glance at him, she saw a little nerve flicking at his temple. Words trembled on her tongue, but she did not speak them and they rode in silence until they were close to the castle that was her home.

'Here I must leave you, Mistress Babette,' he said, his eyes seeking hers. 'If God spares me and I am able, I shall return to you. I pray you, remember me with kindness—and know that I think of you and am grateful for my life.'

'Captain…I thank you,' she whispered, her throat tight. 'I…I shall not forget you.' With that she spurred her horse forward, riding hard towards the castle and across the drawbridge into the outer bailey. She did not look back, even though she sensed that he watched her until she disappeared from his view. 'God protect and keep you—and bring you back to me.'

He could not hear the words, but they were in her heart and would remain until they met again.

Tears caught in her throat and she longed to turn her horse about and ride back to him, but already men had gathered about her and began to exclaim.

'My lady…' Martin, her father's faithful steward, had come rushing down to the court-yard. 'When you were seen I could not believe that it was truly you come back to us. You sent no word?'

'I could not,' she said, lifting her head, all trace of tears gone as he helped her down, looking at her anxiously. 'My uncle no longer felt able to offer me a home and the…kind friends who escorted me home could not wait. I would have had to journey alone had it not been for my friends. Jonas is bringing the wagon with my trunk, but will probably not arrive until the morning, for he knows the drawbridge is raised soon after dusk.'

'Well, I am glad to have you here,' the steward said. 'Have you seen Lord Harvey? Do you know that his wife is here?'

'Yes, I have seen him. I thought he might be here before me. His friend was ill and they intended to make their way here as swiftly as they were able…' She faltered then, 'Will you take me to Lady Alice, please?'

'She is lying in her chamber, which is where

she spends most of her time. I fear she is sickly and I do not know how to comfort her.'

'Poor Martin,' Babette said and laughed. 'Had I known that my brother intended to bring his wife here I should not have deserted you. I shall go up to her and see if I can ease her.'

Suddenly, the burden of doubt had fallen from her shoulders and she was glad to be at home where she was welcome. Martin always sought her advice when any of the household were ill, as he had her mother before she died of a fever taken from nursing one of the villagers. Far from being feared or hated as a witch, the local people had both loved and revered Lady Harvey.

Despite the distress it had caused her to part from Captain Colby with so much left unfinished between them, she knew that she was glad to be safe at home.

Her brother might be angry when he discovered that she had not waited for him to send for her, but perhaps he would understand once she explained that she'd had no choice.

Pushing her doubts away, she went into the castle, feeling the cold strike into her bones. She had forgotten how cold it could be inside its thick stone walls and shivered, holding her cloak about her as she went up the winding steps to the solar she knew would house her brother's wife. At the top, she paused outside and knocked.

'Who is it?' a plaintive voice asked. 'Please go away. My head aches…'

'Perhaps I can ease it,' Babette said and peeped round the door. She saw a pretty, fair-haired woman lying propped up against a pile of feather pillows. Her skin had an unnatural pallor and she did indeed look ill.

Alice looked at her. 'Who are you? Can it be…?' She swung her legs over the bed, looking at Babette with new interest. 'Are you Babette—are you my husband's sister?'

'Yes, indeed I am.'

'Is he with you?' Alice asked eagerly.

'He will be here soon, perhaps tomorrow,' Babette said. 'I came on ahead because he said you needed my company. I can see you are feeling ill—will you tell me what is wrong? Sometimes I can make a cure that will help.'

'I have been feeling so sick and now I have the headache.' A faint colour stained Alice's cheeks. 'Did John tell you that I am with child?'

'Yes, he did.' Babette smiled at her. 'I am so happy for you both—and to know that he is alive and well. I can make a mixture that will ease your sickness and then the headache should go away. Would you like me to do that for you?'

'Yes, please,' Alice said and there was a new animation in her. She smiled and Babette saw why her brother had defied their father to run away with her. 'John said that you would know how to make me feel better.'

'I make only simple cures. There is no mystery or witchcraft in what I do.' Babs looked at her hesitantly and was relieved when she laughed.

'Who would be foolish enough to think you a witch?' she asked and held out her hand. 'Come and sit with me for a moment, tell me where you have been and what made you come home. Was it just for my sake?'

'My uncle is a man of odd but strong views,' Babette said. 'He took it into his head that I… was a bad influence on his daughter and asked me to leave. Some friends were coming this way and escorted me to within sight of the castle.'

'You should have invited them to stay for the night.'

'They had business elsewhere.'

Alice said. 'I think your uncle is a fool, but I am grateful that he sent you home, for I am glad to have you here. I begin to feel better already.'

Babette smiled and took her hand. Some of the colour was returning to Alice's cheeks and she suspected that a large part of her sickness was due to the fact that she was alone in a strange place. The castle had few women servants; it was a place of men, a fortress rather than a comfortable home, and not truly the right home for a lady who looked to be perhaps three or four months gone with child.

'I felt lonely here, too, after my father died. We did not know where John was and I went to visit my aunt for company. She was kind to me and I am fond of my cousin—but my uncle is too stern a man. I am glad to be home with you, Alice, but I should have thought John would take you to the manor house. It is small but pleasant and my mother liked it better than the castle. Though I suppose in these times of war it could not be so well defended.'

'That is why John brought me here.' Alice

sighed. 'He took me first to Brevington Manor, and I liked it there, but he said I could not stay there alone while he was away fighting. I suppose he is right.' Her face lost its animation, her eyes looking large and scared in her pale face. 'I do not know what would happen to me if he…'

Babette understood what troubled her. She was in love with her husband and she feared losing him. It could so easily happen. John might have been wounded instead of Drew— and if she had not been at her uncle's house Drew could have died.

'I cannot promise you that John will not be wounded or even killed,' she said, 'but while I live you will always have a friend in me, Alice.'

'Thank you,' Alice said and embraced her. 'John said you would be good for me and he was right. I shall not be afraid when my child comes now that you are here.'

Babette felt the sting of tears. It had cost her much to choose between her brother and his wife and Captain Colby. She would never have been able to live with herself if she had gone with him and then heard that Alice had gone into a decline.

'We shall love and comfort each other,' she said, kissing Alice's cheek. 'And now I shall make you a pleasant tisane that will make you feel much better. Perhaps tomorrow John and his friend will be here.'

Leaving Alice's room, she went down to her mother's still room. The shelves were packed with jars of cures she had made before she left so that Martin would have something if one of the servants fell sick. There were also bunches of dried herbs and jars with tight-fitting caps that contained other ingredients she used in her tisanes.

She sent a servant to fetch a pan of hot water and mixed her herbs, making a brew that would help Alice feel less sick in the mornings. When it was strong enough, she strained it and added honey to sweeten it, then poured it into a cup and carried it up to her sister-in-law's chamber. She knew that it worked swiftly. By the time her husband returned, Alice should be feeling able to greet him with a smile.

Babette's own heart was aching. She had

parted from the man she loved and did not
know whether she would ever see him again.

'May God protect you and keep you safe,'
she prayed. 'Please come back to me one day—
and do not hate me.'

Chapter Seven

Was he a fool to let her go so easily? James was thoughtful as he turned aside after seeing Babette ride over the drawbridge and into her home. He was certain she was wavering. Had he insisted, would she have thrown caution to the wind and come with him? He had come close to taking her on to his horse and riding away with her—he could have taken her to his home, closed the gates and forgot his duty… forsaking everything for her and love.

Was this feeling burning deep inside him love or merely physical desire? He knew that when she was near he could think only of bedding her, yet when she was in danger his first need had been to take her to safety.

Had he begun to love again? Not in the way he'd worshipped his gentle Jane, but as a man loved the woman who would be his equal, his partner through all the trials of life.

A part of him wanted to return, sweep her on to his horse and ride away!

No, that was foolish, a foolish thought for a weak man. He could never neglect his duty, and her brother would disown her if she wed a man he would name his enemy. She'd had no option but to return to her life and he to his.

It had taken strength to draw back and let her go. He had longed to ride off with her to his home, lock the door and forget there was a war. He wanted to keep her safe from all harm, to spend his life with her and think no more of politics or waging the fight against an unfair King. Yet he knew even as his thoughts rebelled that he could not do it. She must come to him of her own will and for preference with the goodwill of her brother.

James groaned, as he knew how hopeless a cause that might be. Lord Harvey was young and had chosen to fight for his King without giving the causes of the war enough thought. What Englishman in his right mind would condone the kind of taxes that had been forced upon them since Charles I had come to the throne? He thought with regret of the good days when Queen Bess had sat upon the English throne. He was, of course, not old enough to recall it, but his grandfather had revered Gloriana and hated the Scottish King who had taken her place. With his favourites and his petty weaknesses, King James had not served his people well—and his son was a tyrant who believed that he had a divine right to rule as he chose without due recourse to the law or to the people's wishes.

Why did it have to happen in his lifetime? A country torn by civil strife—brother against brother and cousin against cousin. Drew Melbourne had been his friend until they quarrelled over James's decision to stand with Parliament in this tussle. He regretted the breach, but not even for one second had he considered that Drew might be the enemy who had tried to kill him in such a cowardly way.

No, he could think only that it was Jane's brother who hated him so deeply—but he could not think why or what had changed between them. Instead of being united in their grief, as he'd expected, his one-time friend had withdrawn, become distant and cold.

Did he blame him for Jane's death?

Melchet must know that he had nothing to

do with it. He had not even been there when she took ill, though he had hastened to her side.

James frowned. He had never understood how she caught such a terrible fever, but when he held her in his arms that fateful day it had seemed to him that all the life had gone out of her…that she had wanted to die.

No, that was nonsense! She was soon to be married and he knew she loved him for all her shyness and her hesitancy.

Something or someone had distressed her so much that…

James shook his head. He would not let Jane's death torture him again. He had healed slowly, but it had taken a girl with bold eyes to bring him back from that cold place and teach him to live again.

God, how he wished she was here. He toyed with the idea of going back to the castle, of demanding that her brother listen to him. He should never have let her go.

The sound of a pistol shot brought him from his reverie. If he were not mistaken, that sound came from where his men waited for him.

Spurring his horse onwards, he rode towards the sounds of firing and saw that his men were being attacked by a force of perhaps seven

Royalist soldiers. Drawing his sword, he let out a fearsome battle cry and rode straight at them. Whether they thought he was but one of another troop he did not know, but at the sight of him they looked at one another, turned tail and fled towards the woods.

His men fired after them, but the skirmish had been short and ended abruptly due to his timely arrival.

'Thank goodness you came,' his friend Simeon greeted him with a cheerful grin. 'For a moment there I thought they had the better of us.'

'What? There were but seven of them and five of you,' James said and laughed. 'However, I do not think we will stay around to discover if they return with more of their friends. On this occasion I think that discretion is the better part of valour.'

Hearing shots exchanged, John reined in and motioned Drew to do the same. His friend was bent almost double over his horse, so weary that he could not go much farther. John cursed the delay, for he knew that they must reach the castle and the safety of its walls before Drew collapsed. He wished that he had brought a wagon rather than allowing his proud friend to ride, as he'd insisted on doing. Looking at his strained face, he could see that he was at the end of his strength.

As they drew back into the trees, John saw a party of men he knew by their dress were Royalist soldiers—a private troop if he guessed right, undisciplined and led by their lord, who had no idea how to fight. If the fool had spotted a troop of rebels, he should have sent for reinforcements and surrounded them rather than attack with too few men.

Watching them scatter as they rode in what looked to him like a panic, John's mouth twisted. If they were an indication of what to expect from the men loyal to his Majesty, the rebels would win the war. His opinion was confirmed when he saw a smaller band of Parliament soldiers follow and then turn in a different direction.

He frowned as he thought he recognised one or two of them. They were wearing buff coats and wore a yellow band across their chests. He was certain now that they were some of the men he'd seen near his uncle's house. What had brought them this far south? Parliament's strongholds were mostly in the north…unless things had changed while he'd been away.

He waited until they disappeared from view, then, glancing anxiously at his friend, reached over and took hold of the leading rein. Drew had not wanted it, but it had helped several times when he'd been in danger of losing his grip on the reins.

'Not far to go now, Drew,' he said. 'It's a comfortable bed for you this night—you'll be safe when we reach the castle.'

John wished that he'd told his sister to come with them. He'd told her to stay with their uncle because he thought it might be too dangerous for her to accompany them, but he could have done with her skills on the journey. Drew's wound had opened again and he'd had the devil of a job stopping it. The man had lost so much blood it was a wonder he could stay upright.

Thank God the castle was no more than a mile away. John would be glad to be home and to see Alice again. He hoped she would be feeling better than she had when he left her. She'd wept and clung to him then, making him feel bad about leaving her. The sooner he could bring his sister back the better.

* * *

Babette had left Alice to rest while she went to her chamber to change her gown, which was creased and stained from the journey. She would feel much better when she'd had a chance to eat something and a cup of wine would be pleasing—the sweet French wine her father had bought specially for her.

It was as she went down to the Great Hall once more that she heard the commotion and then several men entered at once. They were shouting and calling for wine and she realised that they were some of the Earl's men. It seemed they'd had a skirmish with some rebels and were talking of the fight with relish.

'We should have had them had their reinforcements not arrived,' said one man with a loud voice. He was laughing as he turned and saw Babette and his eyes narrowed. He swept off his hat and bowed to her. 'If it isn't Mistress Babette… Welcome home, my lady.'

Babette did not smile. Captain Richards was not a man she cared for, because she did not like the way his eyes seemed to strip her of her clothes. He had made several advances towards her in the past, which she had rejected as politely as she could. He was in truth one of the reasons that she had written to her aunt and begged to be allowed to stay.

'Thank you, Captain,' she said. 'Did you say you had an encounter with the enemy?' Her heart was beating wildly for she knew it was likely that it had been Captain Colby and his men.

'Aye, that we did. We had them surrounded and would have made short work of them, had a large reinforcement not arrived and charged us. We rode away, for we were not prepared for a large battle.'

Were there other rebel forces in the district? Babette thought there must be, for there had been only six of them and she had counted seven men in the hall.

She hesitated, wanting to ask if any had been killed in the skirmish, but just as she sought a way to frame her question, Martin came up to her, touching her arm discreetly.

'Mistress Babette, your brother has arrived. His friend is ill and needs your services. Will you come now or later?'

'I shall come now,' Babette said. Her supper could wait until later and she did not wish for more of Captain Richard's company. 'Where is the Earl?'

'He is away for a few days. He was called to the King and left the castle in the charge of Captain Richards—though now my lord is home things will change—for the better, I trust.'

Babette guessed from his expression that he cared no more for the Royalist captain than she did. She nodded her head and went with him, following him towards her brother's private chambers. John would want Drew close until he was able to fend for himself again.

'Does my brother know I am here?'

'He was surprised at the news, but thanked God for it, as we all do who know and love you, mistress.'

Babette smiled at him and hurried in his footsteps. She must see what ailed Drew Melbourne before she went to her still room. John had told her he was on the mend, but it sounded as if the journey had exhausted him. What she hoped was that his wound had not opened again, for he had already lost too much blood.

'Well?' John asked as she bent over his friend. 'What do you think, Babs—can you help him?'

'Yes, I think so,' she replied. 'This wound

has not healed as it ought. I fear it must be cauterised. It will hurt him and he may fight us—but you must hold him while I apply the iron.'

'The iron is a fearful thing,' John said. 'Are you sure you can do it?'

'If you and Martin hold him down,' she said. 'It needs a steady hand—and I would not be strong enough to keep him still when the iron burns. He will scream and rear up, but you must hold him while the heat does its work or he could bleed to death.'

'Thank God you were here,' her brother said fervently. 'I wished for you on the journey, but thought it unsafe. Did you travel here with only Jonas for escort?'

'No, I had an escort to protect me,' she said. 'I shall tell you later. I must concentrate on Drew now. This bleeding must be stopped.'

He nodded wordlessly. The red-hot iron was brought. He and Martin held Drew down to the bed, and Babette applied the iron. The stink of burning flesh, his screams and his pain almost unnerved her, but she held it to the putrid flesh for long enough to burn away the infection and stop the slow, persistent drip of blood and pus. When she withdrew it and passed it to the servant, who had turned aside while she did her work, her stomach was heaving and she felt faint and sick.

'You are as white as a sheet,' Martin said. 'Sit down, my lady.'

'I am merely faint from lack of food,' she said with a weary smile. 'I have had a long journey and I made a tisane for Alice before this… I must apply the healing salve to take away some of the pain and then I can eat and drink.'

'I can do that, mistress,' Martin said and took the pot from her. 'Go down to the hall and ask for food.'

'I shall go to my chamber.' She turned to the servant, who had placed the cooling iron in the hearth. 'Please ask Molly to bring food and wine to my chamber.'

He looked at her awkwardly. 'Molly isn't here, mistress. Shall I ask Maigret?'

'Yes, please,' she said, wondering what had happened to her favourite maidservant but too tired to ask.

'Thank you,' John said. 'Rest now, Babs. I must go to Alice now—but I shall see you in the morning.'

Babette inclined her head, but did not look at him. She was so weary that she was not sure she had the strength to eat, except that her stomach was complaining and she felt faint from lack of food.

In the morning Babette felt much recovered. She rose and washed in the water Maigret had brought for her. The girl was helpful and clean in her habits, and Babette thanked her for her service. Just as she was turning away, she recalled that she'd wanted to know about Molly.

'Where is Molly?' she asked. 'Has she gone home? I thought she was happy here?'

'She be happy enough 'til...' Maigret glanced over her shoulder nervously. 'Best I do not say, mistress.'

'You may tell me and no harm will come to you. Did someone upset her?'

''Twas more than upset...' Maigret said and her cheeks went red. 'She told me he forced her, mistress—had her in the shadows as she went about her business. When she threatened to complain to the Earl, he said he would kill her...and so she ran away.'

Her maidservant had been abused by a man and threatened with death to keep his secret! Babette was horrified. Who could have done such a thing? Her father had always been strict about the treatment of the maids and, had he been here, he would have punished the man severely.

'Was it one of the servants?' she asked, then, seeing the fear in the girl's eyes, 'I shall not tell anyone that you told me—but I must know in case it happens again.'

'It be…Captain Richards. But he would deny it, mistress. He would kill me if he knew I'd told you. Molly dared not say so she ran away.'

'Poor Molly. Had I been here I should have helped her somehow.' She nodded, feeling angry and disgusted. She might have known who had so ill treated the maidservant. The way Captain Richards looked at her told her that he would like to treat her in the same way if he dared. 'You may go now, Maigret—and do not worry, he shall not learn of this from me.'

Babette was thoughtful as the girl left her. She knew that she could not go to the Earl, for she had no proof. Captain Richards would deny the charge and without Molly's testimony there was little she could do but bide her time. If she complained to the Earl, he might not listen. She knew he liked the young man, who was always jesting and telling stories in company.

Even if the Earl did believe that the girl had been seduced, he would think her willing. He would say that Molly had invited the captain to flirt with her and, if she got more than she expected, it was her own fault. After all, she was merely a servant.

Babette knew that many men did not respect women as they ought; they might be forced to behave decently with a woman of their own class, but servants or country girls were fair game to some. It made her angry that there was little she could do except bide her time. If he made a mistake, did something that angered the Earl or stepped too far over the line, perhaps she could have him dismissed, but she did not have much hope of it unless his crime was one the Earl would think worthy of such punishment.

At least John was here now. Babette could tell him what she knew. He might not be able to reprimand Richards, because he served the Earl and not Lord Harvey—but perhaps a private word might do more good.

Leaving her chamber, Babette went down into the hall, crossed it to the far tower and climbed the stone steps to the large chamber where her brother kept his private papers and treasure. He had given his bed there to Drew, sleeping next door in his wife's chamber while his sick friend needed the privacy.

Entering, she saw that Drew was alone, propped up against some pillows and looking pale, but fully conscious.

'I hope your shoulder does not pain you too much, sir?'

'It hurts like hell, but I am in your debt, mistress. John told me that I was losing blood again and like to die before you treated me. You have great strength of purpose. I do not think Beth could have done what you did, much as she loves me.'

'Is Beth your wife?'

'She will be when I return to court, if I can persuade her father to let us wed,' he said and smiled. 'We have loved each other for a while, but my father hoped for other things. I could not wed her until… He died recently and I no longer feel bound by what he would have agreed. But her father has taken against me, perhaps because I delayed.'

Babette looked at him steadily. 'You need feel no awkwardness as far as I am concerned, sir. I know our fathers sought to make a match between us—but I do not expect or wish for it.'

Drew looked relieved. 'Thank you, mistress, that is most generous. I confess I did feel awkward when I knew how much you had done for me. My father encouraged yours to think I would agree to the match. I did not elope with Beth, for she would not…but she is the woman I love and I shall wed no other.'

'Then you should wed her as soon as you are able,' Babette said and smiled at him. 'You owe me nothing—and especially not marriage. Besides, there is someone I like well.'

'Then I am happy to hear it,' he said. 'But if there is ever anything I can do for you, you have only to ask. I am in your debt, though you deny it.'

Babette shook her head. She had done only what she would do for any man in desperate need. Drew was her brother's friend and she was glad to have helped him.

'For the moment I lack for nothing,' she said and then frowned. Perhaps if she asked Drew to help in the matter of Captain Richards he might do so, but even as she considered the door opened and her brother entered.

'Good morning, Sister. I trust you are feeling better?'

'I was merely tired and hungry last night,' she replied. 'I am quite well, thank you.'

'Alice tells me how much you have helped her. She is more like herself again—and so glad to have your company.'

'I shall go to her when I have changed this dressing.'

'I can do that,' John said. 'It was a miracle you got here—who did you say escorted you?'

'Our uncle's cousin,' Babette said. 'He was ready to leave and—and Uncle Matthew did not want me in the house. He accused me of witchcraft because I dug a ball from a man's shoulder and bound him so that he did not bleed to death.'

'Good grief! What kind of a man is he? What would he have had you do—leave the poor devil to bleed to death?'

'Perhaps. He would have sent for the doctor, but you may recall that Mother did not trust physicians. She said they killed more than they cured through infection. However, I think my uncle an honest man, but with strange fears,' Babette replied. 'It does not matter. I am here now and all is well.'

'Yes…' John frowned at her, and she knew he had guessed that the man who had escorted her home was the rebel captain who had been wounded. 'Go to Alice now, Babs. We shall speak of this again.'

He did not want to accuse her in front of Drew Melbourne. Babette was glad to escape, even though she knew the reckoning would come later.

'A Puritan, Babs?' John looked at her half in anger and half in bewilderment. 'I should not have thought you would put your trust in such a man.'

'He was not a Puritan,' she said, her cheeks warm as she faced him proudly. 'I thought him honest—a man of principle and beliefs, to which he held true. He argues that the King imposed unfair taxes. I do not say that I share his views, but he was a generous, courteous man. Had he not offered his escort I should have had to make my own way, for Uncle Matthew would not have me in his house another day.'

'Curse the man!' John said, his face like thunder. 'How dared he treat you so? I swear that I shall make him pay for this one day, Babs. To treat you so scurvily—and after you had saved his cousin's life!'

'He was unfair. Aunt Minnie did not like it, but there was naught she could do—she is afraid of him. Angelina cried. She wanted to come to me, but he would never let her.'

'A plague on his house,' John said. 'The man is a superstitious fool. To say such things of our mother…it is a good thing you left.' He nodded. 'I thought I saw Colby when we approached the castle. He and his men sent some Royalists flying, though they were the larger troop. If all our enemies were like him…' He shook his head. 'Rupert complains that some of our troops are ill disciplined and inclined to flee at the slightest setback. I fear he may be right. They have enthusiasm in plenty, but no discipline.' He was thoughtful for a moment, his expression sombre. 'Very well, I shall not scold you, but I do not like the thought of you being at that rebel's mercy.'

'Captain Colby was a gentleman, John. I was quite safe with him, for he was honourable and would not take advantage of the situation. Indeed, I think him not so different from you. There are things that happened in the Star Chamber. I do not think Father would have approved…'

'He would have been loyal to the King no

matter what,' John said. 'It is not for us to question what his Majesty chooses to do—I dare say he has his reasons for all he does.'

Babette saw the doubts in his eyes. 'What troubles you, Brother? I know there is something, though you love the King well.'

'Stafford's impeachment. He was a good, loyal man and Father's friend. I did not like that he was made a scapegoat. But that does not mean I will accept criticism of the King's decisions. Those rogues in Parliament forced him to it. I am certain he has regretted that he allowed them to dictate to him.'

'Yes, I dare say he was forced into an act he did not like,' she agreed. 'Perhaps it was that that caused him to set up his standard and begin this war. I am for his Majesty, as you are, John—but I think you might like Captain Colby if you knew him.'

'Perhaps I might if we met at a different time,' John agreed. 'But you are not thinking of anything more than a fleeting acquaintance, I hope? Father should have arranged your marriage a year since, but now I am here there will be friends I can bring to your attention, men you will like as much as that rebel captain.'

Babette did not think it likely, for he had

touched her heart as no other ever had, but she would not argue with her brother. Frowning, she said, 'As long as they are not like Captain Richards.'

'What has he done to distress you?'

'I dislike the way he looks at me—and he forcibly seduced one of my maids. I was away and she did not dare accuse him to the Earl, so she ran away.'

'How do you know this is true? She might have encouraged him.'

'Molly was not like that,' she said and saw his frown darken. 'She was a happy, friendly girl, but she did not set her cap at any—though I think her family expected her to marry a yeoman farmer in time.'

'You are right. Molly was not that kind of girl,' John agreed. 'If I knew for sure that he had forced her, I should not tolerate him here.'

'Believe me, it is true even though I have no proof,' Babette said. 'He is a bragging bully and he makes me feel uncomfortable. I have seen him look at me in such a way—if he had the chance…'

'He would not dare lay a finger on you!'

'No, but I have seen him look at me as if it is in his mind.'

'I will see if I can have him sent on a mission for his Majesty,' John said. 'Carlton favours him, but if I make it seem a mark of esteem mayhap he will agree to it.'

'We should go on much better without him. You saw his men flee from the rebel troop and yet he bragged that they were winning until set upon by a much larger force.'

'A coward and a bully.' John looked angry. 'He is not the only one to be met with in his Majesty's army. Were he in Rupert's troop he would soon learn the error of his ways—but it is not easy to get rid of these braggarts. They swagger and boast and most believe them.'

'Do nothing that would bring harm to you,' she said. 'But if you could find a way to send him from the castle I should be grateful.'

John smiled at her and nodded. 'I shall try to arrange it,' he promised, 'and do not worry. I would have you stay here with Alice until she has given birth, but I shall not forget you, Babs. A marriage shall be arranged for you.'

'Do not let it concern you yet. I am in no hurry and I think Alice needs me until you can be with her. She was fretting for you and that brought on her headaches. Now that I have given her something for the sickness she should be better, but I would not leave her here alone.'

'You are thoughtful,' her brother said, and she turned away, not wanting him to know that she did not wish him to arrange a marriage with one of his friends. In time, perhaps, she would wish for a husband and a home of her own, but for the moment there was only one man in her mind.

She wondered where Captain Colby was and what he had done after he left her. How long would it be before they met again? With this terrible civil war inflaming the country, it might be months or years before he was free to come to her. She felt a wave of despair flow over her, but then raised her head defiantly.

She would devote herself to making Alice comfortable and ease her through the pain of childbed, and she would care for her servants and the sick in the village as she'd always done. Perhaps one day she would find happiness, but until that day arrived she must do whatever her friends and family asked of her.

Chapter Eight

Was she still at the castle? Was she well—was she happy? The thoughts of Babette chased through James's mind as he looked out of the window. They were in a manor house belonging to Lord Manchester for a conference before the spring and summer campaign began. The winter had been spent mostly in training and moulding the men into a force of determined fighting men, but they would be on the move again as soon as there was news that King Charles had left Oxford, where he had spent most of the year.

'The King must be brought to battle,' Cromwell said. 'Our men are ready to fight and a skirmish here or there is nothing. We need a decisive battle that will turn the tide of the conflict.'

'How can we force him to fight if he insists on staying put?' Lord Manchester said, sprawling in his chair, a cup of wine to hand. 'While he continues to evade us he has the upper hand.'

'We must attack Royalist strongholds,' Cromwell said. 'Lay siege to them—rout out these smug men who laugh at us from the safety of their castles.'

'I cannot see what good it would do unless the King happened to be in the castle,' Manchester said in a bored tone. 'No, we must wait until the appointed time and meet as gentlemen on the field of battle—and now I wish you goodnight.'

'That fool…' Cromwell muttered as the stout lord heaved himself from his chair and went out. 'What do you think, Colby? I see no point in petty skirmishes with no outcome or point to victory. I have trained my men and they are ready for battle. If I were in command…'

'You should have the overall command of the army. Lord Manchester's heart is only half in it. Essex is a brilliant general, but I think if his Majesty would come halfway to meet him he would go back to the old way and forget all that we have strived for.'

'Over my dead body.' Cromwell sighed. 'He is not the only one, James. Sometimes I think I waste my time and would have done better to take ship for the New World.'

'If you did that, we should surely lose the war,' James said. 'I wish that it had never come to this, but it has and I believe you may be right to think we must harry them, lay siege to their strongholds and make the King come to battle. We need a decisive win if we are to finish this conflict and bring Charles Stuart to his senses.'

'Yes.' Cromwell nodded. 'I have men ready to fight as and where I direct. We have called ourselves the Ironsides and I think the Royalists will not find it so easy to beat us as formerly. I believe I shall begin the attacks and see where it leads. You were recommended to me because of your successful foraging— will you join me? I need a resourceful man like you.'

'Yes, sir, gladly,' James said, for he admired this man with his stern looks and plain speaking. 'I believe the Royalists are strongest in the south, but I do not know what you had in mind.'

'We shall make our move before the summer is out,' Cromwell promised. 'I shall not tolerate another winter of stalemate. I want a decisive battle.'

James nodded. He said goodnight to his commander and retired to his own quarters. Was it almost a year since he had seen Mistress Babette? The time between had been spent at first in battles up and down the country—some of them important, others merely skirmishes—and then relentless training in the colder months. Now it was spring again and Cromwell was impatient to be on the move.

James had not forgot the sweet lady with the bold eyes who had saved his life, but it had been impossible to find an opportunity to see her. He had written to her several times, but had no way of getting his letters to her. Any courier he sent to the castle would have been seen as a spy and a letter from him might have caused her to be named a traitor. At times he despaired of ever seeing her again—and the hopes he'd had of a marriage between them seemed no more than dust blowing in the wind.

The war seemed to drag on and went nowhere. The King had won several battles, but then a setback had sent him scurrying to Oxford, where he'd spent much of his time since. Essex had won his share of the conflicts, but it was as Cromwell said: a stalemate with neither side scoring a decisive victory. They must unsettle the Royalists somehow and perhaps attacking their manors and homes would bring them to battle. Prince Rupert had taken Bristol and was holding the crucial port. The city must be put under siege, which would tie up a portion of their forces, but while the Royalists held such an important access to the sea they were too well supplied.

James groaned with frustration. Would this war never be over? Would he ever be free to go in search of the woman whose eyes haunted him?

And did she ever think of him?

She was alone in the mist and something in the thick blanket of fog was so menacing that it terrified her. She knew that if she did not run away whatever was there would come and seize her. Crying a name out loud, she sat up with a start and opened her eyes.

She was in her room at the castle and it was in darkness. There was no mist, nothing menacing her—only the loneliness she had felt more and more as the months passed.

'James, where are you?' she whispered in

the darkness, and a tear trickled down her cheek. She had thought of the gallant captain who had escorted her home so often through the lonely winter. Now it was spring again and the months went by so slowly, for there was no sign of the war ending—no reason to think that she would ever see him again. 'You promised…you promised to return.'

Dashing the tears from her cheeks, Babette got out of bed and pulled on a warm wrapping gown. There was no point in crying for something she could not have. She had chosen duty and, if her duty seemed hard at times, Alice ungrateful and her life unrewarding, she had only herself to blame.

She had hoped that a letter might come, but she knew it would be almost impossible for James to contact her—and yet she'd looked for a letter and been disappointed so many times.

'When shall I see you again?' she asked, but no answer came.

Standing to look down at the courtyard as the first rosy fingers of dawn appeared, she felt her loneliness wash over her. The castle was not truly her home now, for it belonged to John and Alice was his wife. She made use of Babette when she needed her, but made it clear that she was the chatelaine here. When John returned from the war, it would be time for Babette to leave—but that meant she must marry, for a woman of her class had no other choice.

Unless James came for her, she would be forced to wed a man of her brother's choice.

No, she would not wed a man she could not love. Closing her eyes, she remembered the scent of James Colby and that ride through the woods when he held her. She recalled the touch of his hands and the way he had looked at her, and her body ached with need. She longed to be in his arms to be kissed and… Her cheeks burned as she became aware of her wanton thoughts.

She must put such thoughts away, for it was not seemly—and yet she burned for his touch and thought of him every night before she slept.

'You are so lucky, Alice,' Babette said, looking down at the chubby boy lying in his cradle. His legs had been released from the swaddling that had been imposed on him for the first few months of his life and he kicked out with glee, clearly loving his new freedom. 'He is a lovely child.'

'Yes, he is beautiful,' Alice said. 'John was so proud of him when he visited last month.' She sighed deeply. 'When will this awful war be over, Babs? I want John to come home to us. I know he has been lucky so far, but for how long can it continue? I am so tired of being cooped up here in this wretched place—it is almost like being in prison. If John is killed, I shall not bear it.'

'You must not let your fears cloud your mind,' Babette said. 'Until the war ends none of us can be certain what will happen…but at least John visits as often as he can.'

'Why must he volunteer for these dangerous missions when he could stay safe within the castle?'

'We may not be safe here for much longer,' Babette said. 'The Earl of Carlton told us that several stout manor houses have fallen of late and towns and castles are vulnerable to these attacks. They say Cromwell's new force is the most powerful army yet seen in this country.'

'Do not say so,' Alice said and shivered, looking down at her child. 'They say the Puritans stick babies on their pikes.'

'You had that from Captain Richards,' Babette said and frowned. Her brother had succeeded in sending the captain away, but he had returned recently, bearing a message from his Majesty. 'I should not take too much notice of what he says, Alice. I do not think the rebels are such evil brutes. In battle men die, but I doubt very much that the rebels would kill innocent babies in the way he described.'

'Captain Richards would not lie to me,' Alice said and smirked. 'He is always so gallant, and he talks to me of the court—' She broke off as they heard the roar of cannon, looking at one another in fright. 'What is that?'

'I do not know.' Babette went to the small window to look down at the courtyard below. Men were running back and forth and shouting. It was a scene of total chaos and she knew that her worst fears had come to pass. The castle was under siege. 'I think we are being attacked.'

Alice gave a little scream. She snatched up her baby and held him to her breast, a look of fear in her eyes.

'They will kill us all!'

'They have to break down our defences first,' Babette said, but felt a spasm of nerves in her stomach. 'Do not lose all hope yet, Alice. When John hears he will bring a force to relieve us—as they have at other houses and cities.'

'God pray that he comes in time,' Alice said. Her eyes were dark with fear, which Babette knew was as much for her child as herself. 'What will they do to us if…?'

Babette put an arm about her, trying to comfort her. She, too, was anxious, because she had thought the Roundheads, as they were now often called because of the peculiar-shaped helmets they had taken to wearing, would not bother with a castle that was of little strategic value. It was understandable that the important port of Bristol should be fought over, as were several important cities, but she had hoped Cromwell's men would pass them by.

'I shall go to the Earl,' she said. 'He will know whether the castle may be defended and for how long.'

Leaving Alice to nurse her child, Babette went down to the Great Hall. Here there were signs of chaos as the servants ran hither and thither like headless chickens. No one seemed to know what was happening and it was obvious that no one was in command. Since there was no sign of the Earl, she went out into the courtyard. Her steward was directing men to fill buckets of water. As she saw the ball of flaming pitch fly over the wall into a stack of straw, she understood the meaning of his actions. She went up to him.

'Forgive me, but Lady Alice is frightened for her child. Where is the Earl? Can the castle stand such an attack?'

'You should not be out here,' Martin said. 'You could be injured, my lady. Please go back inside.'

'Where is the Earl?'

Martin pointed up to the battlements. 'He is directing our defence himself, my lady.'

Babette looked. She could plainly see the Earl directing the efforts of his men and encouraging them to stand firm in the face of this determined assault. Surely he should have left this to his captains? She frowned, for the Earl was in charge here and without him... Even as the thought crossed her mind, she heard the roar of cannon and a hole was blown in the castle wall just below where the Earl was standing. The shock blew him and the men nearest to him off their feet and masonry came falling down on them.

'The Earl is wounded...' the cry went up, and as Babette watched some men picked him up and brought him down the narrow stone steps to the courtyard where she stood. She saw that he was badly hurt, blood pouring from a chest injury and another to his head.

'Bring him to his chamber,' she commanded. 'I shall do what I can for him, but he may not survive.'

Why, why had he been so foolish? He was a brave man, but now the castle was in the command of the most senior captain and that was Captain Richards. Babette went quickly ahead to the Earl's chamber, where she threw back the covers and instructed that he be placed down gently. Bending over him, she looked and saw that he was still conscious, though in great pain.

'You cannot save me, Mistress Babette,' he told her in a rasping voice. 'Without me, the castle may fall. You and Lady Alice must take the child and go through the secret passage. It leads from my chamber and ends in the church in the village. Go quickly, for I fear if you wait it may be too late. The enemy are too strong and help may not come in time.'

'I cannot leave you,' Babette said. 'I shall bind your wounds. We have not lost the battle yet.'

'Please go or I have failed…' He closed his eyes, a tear sliding down his cheek.

Babette bent over him, pressing a pad of clean linen to the wound in his chest. She saw from the mangled flesh that whatever she did would be useless. No man could survive such injuries. Indeed, even as she tried to bind him, she saw the colour ebb from his face and knew that he had slipped away.

What ought she to do? Would it be better to wait and see if the enemy could be held off? Surely the castle was strong enough to withstand several days of determined attack. Hearing the roar of cannon again, she hurried from the Earl's chamber, intending to go to Alice and ask her if she wished to try escaping through the secret passage.

Babette's father had shown her the secret many years ago, though he'd laughed and boasted that it would never be necessary to use it. She had believed herself totally safe here, but now…

Seeing Captain Richards coming towards her, she stopped, asking him the question on her mind, 'What is happening? How long can we hold out?'

'The Earl is needed,' Richards said. 'Without him the men are anxious. He must come back and give them heart. Most are for surrendering.'

Babette sensed his fear and knew that he thought surrender the only way. 'I fear the Earl is dead, sir. You are in command now.'

She saw the start of fear and knew that, left to himself, he would surrender rather than fight to the death. He talked well, but at heart was a coward who thought only of his own pleasures.

'I am not sure how long we can hold out,' he said. 'Ten men have died already and they are too strong for us. They have fearful machines of war—and if we fight on we may all die.'

'Lady Alice and the child must be safe,' Babette said. 'There is a way of escape—if you can hold out for a few hours?'

'A way of escape?' She saw hope flare in his eyes. 'Where—how?'

'A secret passage in the Earl's chamber. You must promise me to hold out for long enough for us to escape... Please, for Lady Alice and the child?'

'Very well. I shall tell the men that the Earl is merely resting,' he said. 'We can hold for a few hours.'

'Thank you, sir. I am grateful.'

Babette left him and hurried to Alice's chamber. There was no choice now—they must go quickly before the castle fell to this determined assault, though why its defences should have proved so ineffective she did not know.

Alice looked into the darkness of the tunnel. She was carrying the child wrapped in shawls, while the two maidservants carried bundles of clothing and some food, which would be needed for their journey. Babette carried a bundle containing Alice's jewels and some gold John had left in her charge, also her own few trinkets. It was heavy and she'd looked with regret at her father's alabaster bowl, for she could not take it with her. Jonas had brought a pistol and some other bits and pieces stuffed into a sack, which he carried over his shoulder. He had not wanted to leave the castle until she reminded him that it was his duty to look after Lord Harvey's heir.

They had decided they must try to reach Brevington Manor, which was in the county of Hampshire and some leagues hence. Perhaps they would be able to buy horses for themselves—or perhaps a wagon. As yet Babette had had no time to think what she must do. She was anxious to remove her sister-in-law and the child from danger, though a part of her felt guilty at leaving when she knew some of the men were wounded and needed help.

Martin had come to her as she prepared to leave. When she told him of her fears for the wounded, he brushed them aside.

'Our men have fought for your sake and the Lady Alice. Her child will one day be Lord Harvey. Your duty is to take them to safety. I have the cures and salves you made for us, mistress. I shall do what I can for the injured, though some will die…whether you are here or not.'

Babette knew he was right. Alice was nervous of escaping through a dark, secret tunnel and would never have the courage to go alone. Besides, the journey would be dangerous and she could not desert her now.

'It looks so dark…' Alice said fearfully. 'There are cobwebs and spiders.'

'I shall go first and break through them.' Babette held her lanthorn high, the yellow light of the candle lifting the pitch-black of the tunnel. She waved her bundle at the cobweb that had spread across the narrow passage and saw several spiders go scurrying. A shudder went through her, for she liked them no more than Alice, but there was no choice but to leave this way. It was up to her to go first, because she was the only one who knew how to work the lever that would open a door into the ancient church in the village. 'Come, dearest one, have courage. It is better than facing enemy soldiers, is it not?'

Hearing shouting and cheering, she glanced over her shoulder. Surely the castle had not surrendered already? Captain Richards had promised to hold out for a few hours, but even as she looked back, Martin came into the chamber.

'Go quickly, my lady,' he urged. 'Captain Richards put up the white flag and the enemy are within the gates.'

'You must come with us,' Alice said, but he shook his head.

'Nay. The door must be secured from here— and I shall be needed here to protect the vulnerable if I can. Go before they come.'

Alice and the two maids followed Babette into the passage and the door was shut from within the Earl's chamber. Since it could not be opened from inside, they now had no choice but to escape through the church.

Captain Richards had made terms in the hope of saving his own skin, Babette thought angrily. Indeed, it surprised her that he had not insisted on escaping with her through the passage. Her lips curled in scorn, for she knew that had her father been in the castle, he would have fought to the last and his men would have stood with him. The Earl had been a brave man, but foolhardy, and with his death there had been no one to rally the men or give them a reason to fight on.

'It's cold in here,' Alice said. 'How far is it, Babs?'

'Not long now,' Babette said. 'Have courage, dearest.'

'I'm trying…' Alice made a little sound of disgust. 'Something just ran over my foot.'

'Do not think about it,' Babette said. 'We must get your son to safety—think only of him, Alice.'

'I'm not sure I can bear this,' she moaned as something brushed against her face. 'I can't breathe…'

'It is just fear,' Babette told her. 'Take a deep breath. Another few minutes and we shall be there.'

Babette did not tell her of her own fears—

which were that there might be Roundhead soldiers stationed in the village.

'Marston's force is attacking Haverston Castle,' Cromwell said. 'It is well defended and I think he may need reinforcements. I want you to lead a supply troop and back him up, James.'

James felt the pulse start to beat rapidly at his right temple, and his fists curled at his sides. He had feared this day might come, for this new policy of attacking randomly and forcing the Royalists from their strongholds had always meant that Mistress Babette might one day be in danger. He had hoped that he might be a part of the attacking force so that he could protect them and prayed that he might not arrive too late. Yet from what he had seen from a distance the castle was stout and ought to hold out against a siege of some weeks.

He saluted his commander, then went to assemble the supply wagons and gather his troop. If Captain Marston was dug in for a long siege, he would need these extra supplies of ammunition and food. The Earl of Carlton was known to be a brave and stubborn man, though whether he had the skill to defend the castle was an unknown factor.

James could not help wondering about Babette and her sister-in-law. Mistress Babs had told him that her brother's wife was with child, which was her reason for returning to the castle. That child must have been born some months previously. Were they all still at the castle or had they gone to Oxford to join the King? Had he been Babette's brother and on the King's side, he would have taken his wife and sister there—in times of war castles were not the place for women and children, for they were liable to be attacked. Oxford was too well defended to invite attack at the moment, though if Cromwell had his way the day when they would be strong enough to march against it was not so far distant—if, of course, they made the advances they hoped this summer.

James's mind returned to his present problem. Marston was not a monster. He would surely give the women a free passage and let them leave in safety, as he would the men-at-arms—if they surrendered on honourable terms.

Yet even if they were allowed to leave the castle they would be defenceless women alone in troubled times. He believed Lord Harvey had another house. Would they try to go there?

James frowned. If he were in time, he would help escort them to safety, but…

He pushed the anxious thoughts from his mind. From here he could do nothing. He must take his men to Marston's aid and see what the situation was when he arrived.

'Thank God we are out of that wretched tunnel,' Alice exclaimed when they stood in the church. They had come up in the vestry and were busy brushing the dirt from their clothes and hair when the vicar entered. He looked shocked to see them and then hurried forward to greet them.

'Lady Harvey, Mistress Babette,' he said. 'How glad I am to see you. We knew that the castle was under attack, but we thought it would hold out for much longer.'

'Had my father or brother been there we might have held for at least two or three weeks,' Babette said with a touch of bitterness. 'The Earl was killed in the first attack and his subordinates could not hold the men to their posts.'

'I am sorry to hear that Carlton was killed,' the vicar said, shaking his head. 'Lord Harvey would have fought to the last, I know. I do not think these Roundheads would have beaten him so easily—but what of you? Where will you go?'

'I think we must go to my brother's manor,' Babette said. 'Tell me, are there soldiers in the village?'

'They are all at the castle for the moment, though I think some may return soon. You should leave at once, for I think they will look for you once they know you have fled.'

'Yes, we shall go. Do you know of anyone who would let us buy a wagon and horses?'

'You may have my own cart, Mistress Babette—and I need no payment. Your father was a good patron of the church and of me. I fear I cannot let you have my riding horse, for I need it for my work in the parish—but the cart will not be needed until the harvest and one of my neighbours will lend me a cart if it is still of use to you by then.'

'I shall send it back to you with Jonas, once we are settled at the manor,' she promised. 'Your kindness will not be forgot, sir.'

'I wish that I could do more, mistress—but my duty is here with my flock, and you have Jonas to protect you.'

'Yes, thank you,' Babette said. 'Please have

your cart made ready. We shall stay here in the church until we can safely leave.'

The vicar nodded and went out swiftly. He returned in a very few minutes, saying that the cart was ready. 'I am delighted to tell you that my curate has offered his own horse for your use, Mistress Babette. He says it is but a docile nag and not fit—but it will carry either you or Lady Alice.'

'I shall ride in the cart with my son,' Alice said. 'Babette must take the horse.'

'But what of Mr Smith—how will he manage his parish work?'

'He says the Lord gave him legs to walk and he will walk as Jesus did himself. Perhaps I ought to do the same—but my legs will not bear me too far these days.'

'No, sir.' Babette smiled at him. 'You have done more than we could have expected. Your cart and the curate's horse will be sufficient for our needs.'

'Mistress…' The maidservant Janice looked at her, a self-conscious expression in her eyes. 'Will you forgive me if I do not come with you? I should not like to go so far from my home. With your permission I shall stay here in the village and wed my promised lad.'

'If that is your wish, Janice. Maigret—do you also wish to stay?'

'Nay, Mistress Babette. I shall come with you wherever you go.'

'Then you will come and Janice will stay. It will be one less for the cart to carry.' She slipped her hand into the purse at her waist and took out a silver coin, pressing it into Janice's hand. 'This is for your marriage gift. I bear you no ill will for wishing to stay.'

The girl's eyes filled with tears as she turned her head away, shamed that she had let her mistress down. Babette had no time to comfort her. Jonas was urging them to leave and she followed him outside to the cart and horses. The nag the curate had loaned her was worse than the old grey cob Jonas normally rode. Babette longed for her own mare and felt regret at having to leave her in the castle stables, but there was no way she could have brought the horse with her.

Lifting her head proudly, she allowed Jonas to help her into the saddle. Resolutely, she led the way from the church, down a narrow lane and towards the road that led towards Hampshire and London. Brevington Manor stood beside some sweet water meadows and was a lovely old house. She could only pray that it was still standing and that they would reach it in safety.

They had escaped the dangers of the castle, but who knew what awaited them on their journey?

'You say the Earl surrendered after the second attack?' James asked incredulously. 'But you could not have breached these walls so quickly.' He'd seen little sign of damage as he and his men rode up, apart from one hole in the wall that had brought down a part of the turret.

'The Earl was up on the ramparts and killed in the first round of cannon fire—and his subordinate surrendered on terms favourable to himself and his men. We were to let them lay down their arms and then march out, which I was happy to do, for we are not murderers.'

'No, for we should betray the cause we fight for—justice and freedom for all.' James looked at him anxiously. 'What of the ladies? Did they go with the men?'

'We saw no sign of ladies…were there women here?'

'I heard as they escaped through a tunnel,' one of the soldiers said. 'The servants here were talking amongst themselves. Martin, the steward, ordered them to be quiet. He has stayed here, tending the wounded and trying to keep things in order.'

'I would see him,' James said. 'Excuse me, do you know where I may find him?'

He was frowning as he went in search of the steward, who had so bravely stayed to tend the wounded. Where had Babette and her sister-in-law gone? Did they not know how dangerous it was to roam the countryside alone? Not everyone was as gallant as Captain Marston. Renegades from either side could set them upon them… He must discover which way they had gone and go after them for their protection. If it was to the manor at Brevington, he would see them safely settled before he returned to his duty.

'Try to keep the child quiet,' Babette hissed as it whimpered. 'If they see us, we know not what they will do.'

They had hidden in the trees twice thus far, once to avoid a troop of Roundhead soldiers and a second time when they saw a band of gypsies. This time Jonas had caught sight of riders behind them and ordered them all into the woods to hide.

'He won't stop crying,' Alice said. 'He needs to feed, I think, or perhaps his napkin is soiled.'

'Hush!' Babette warned as she heard the sound of men's voices, but as if to spite her, the little boy let out a mighty wail and started to scream as loudly as his lungs would allow. 'Oh, no...' she moaned as the men stopped and looked towards them.

'I heard something, Captain,' one of the men said. 'It sounds like a child.'

'Yes, it does.' The man in charge got down from his horse and moved towards them. Babette braced herself. Her bundle was heavy and she tensed, ready to swing it down on his head if he tried to grab her or Alice, but then as he came towards her she saw his face and gave a cry of relief. 'Captain Colby—is it truly you?'

'Mistress Babs?' he said, and she saw the gladness and the relief she felt echoed in his eyes. 'We have been following you for hours. Thank God we found you! Are you all safe?'

'Yes, thank you,' she cried, and her emotions were so tangled and so fierce that she felt the tears start to her eyes, though she brushed them away. Her heart was racing wildly. James was here. She had thought of him, longed for him so many times and now he was here with her, offering her his protection. Was she dreaming? Had God truly been so kind to her? 'The castle surrendered. We escaped and we are trying to reach Brevington Manor.'

'Yes, I thought that must be your intention,' he said. 'You should not have run away. Marston does not make war on women and children—he would have sent you out with an escort of your own men.'

Babette's lips curled in scorn. 'The same men who surrendered a sound castle for fear of their own lives? I think I would rather take my chances alone.'

James smiled oddly. 'I think the Earl died bravely, but foolishly. Had he directed the men from a safer position you might still have been in the castle—but as it is I must insist that you allow us to escort you to your home.'

'I thank you, sir,' Babette said and turned to Alice. 'Come, Sister, this is the gentleman I told you of. Captain Colby saw me safely home when my uncle turned me from his house. I would trust him more than any man I know other than my brother.'

'I give you my word that you and your child will be safe with me, Lady Harvey,' James said. 'I fight for freedom and justice for all men—and that includes any lady I meet, whether she be for Parliament or the King.'

Alice inclined her head, clearly impressed with the captain's open manners. 'Then I thank you, sir. I do not like this war and wish it were over. We shall accept your safe passage and thank you kindly for it.'

'Then come out from the trees and we shall be on our way. I know that there is a band of renegades in the area—they fight for no cause but their own and should be hung. I was anxious in case they might discover you before we could and was afraid for your safety—but they will not harm you now.'

Babette led her horse forward. James put his hands about her waist and lifted her to the saddle. She felt herself tremble and knew it was not from fear. His nearness was making her wild with joy. She longed to be alone with him, to be held in his arms and kissed—and she knew that if he asked her again she would not refuse to be his wife.

The months apart had been long and lonely. Babette did not wish to be parted from him again—at least she did not wish to do so without an understanding that they would marry as soon as it was possible. She could only hope that the months had not changed him and that he cared for her as she did for him—but her heart sang as she looked into his face. He had set out in search of her as soon as he knew she was in danger. He must care for her a little... surely he did?

Chapter Nine

They travelled for the rest of that day, Babette feeling happier than she had for many
months. Alice looked at her oddly from time
to time, and she sensed that her sister-in-law
felt uncomfortable at travelling with someone she thought of as an enemy, even though
she had been glad to accept their escort. Alice
would have much preferred to travel with a
Royalist party, and Babette guessed that she
regretted escaping through the passage. Had
they waited they might have had their own
men about them—and Babette sensed that
Alice liked the boastful but charming Captain Richards. Babette herself was comfortable and happy to be with men she trusted, but
Alice looked on edge.

'Do not be anxious, dearest,' she whispered to her brother's wife. 'We are as safe with these gentlemen as we should be with a Royalist troop.'

Alice nodded, but the doubts were in her eyes. 'You seem so comfortable with them, Babs—may I ask what this man is to you?'

Babette drew a deep breath, then, 'If he asks me, I shall wed him. I have had nothing but kindness at his hands and…I love him.'

'Have you told him?'

Babette shook her head, a faint flush in her cheeks. 'I shall do so when he speaks. He asked once, but I turned him down, because my duty was to you and my brother. But when we reach Brevington you will be safe and perhaps—'

'You would not leave us?' Alice looked at her in alarm. 'Please promise me that you will not desert us—at least until the war is over and John comes home.'

Alice was asking her to put aside her own hopes of happiness for her sake. She was not sure that she could oblige her this time. The past year had been so long and lonely, with no word from the man she loved—and she did love him with all her heart. She had known it the moment they met again, had known it in her heart for many months.

'I am not sure,' she said. 'If Captain Colby speaks to me, I shall ask him what his intentions are. Perhaps an understanding will be enough, but it must be for him to decide.'

Alice turned her face away, and Babette knew that she was angry. She had become accustomed to leaning on Babette and she would be forced to order her servants and care for her child alone if she were to leave. The prospect did not please her. For a moment Babette felt that she was being torn apart by her loyalty to one and her love for the other—but she had given a year of her life to Alice and she could not know if her chance of happiness would come again. Alice needed her, but she did not always show affection when they were together.

Babette spurred her horse to ride at Captain Colby's side. 'Where do you go when you have seen us safe at Brevington, sir?'

'To my own manor of Colby,' he replied and his eyes were soft as they dwelled on her face. 'I hope you will see it for yourself one day, mistress.'

'I should like to see it very much,' she said,

her eyes meeting his bravely, though she trembled inwardly. 'Very much.'

His look intensified, his eyes smoky with an emotion she could not determine. 'Can it be… Have you changed your mind, Babs? The question I asked you before. If I were to ask you again…?'

Now her cheeks felt as if they burned. She sent a shy smile winging his way and dipped her head, willing him to understand. 'I found these past months hard to bear with no news.'

'I wrote many letters,' he said, 'but there was no way to make sure they were delivered to you. Had I sent a messenger I doubt he would have been permitted through the gates—and you might have been thought a traitor by some.'

'I did not write to you, but I sent you messages in my thoughts.'

Were her eyes saying all the words she dared not say? Perhaps they were, for his smile deepened, caressing her, giving her cause to hope.

'The war goes on,' he said, 'but I would have an understanding with you, Babs. You are the lady I honour above all others and I would have you to wife—even if I have to wait until the end of the war to claim you.'

'Perhaps we need—' She'd been about to say they need not wait, when a shout from one of his men alerted him. A scout had reported seeing a large party of soldiers ahead, but they were not certain on whose side they fought.

'I do not know the banner, sir. I think it may be a local trained band, but whether it be for the King or Parliament I do not know.'

'We shall go across the fields and avoid them,' James said and frowned. 'Forgive me, ladies, but I would avoid these men. If their colours are unknown, they could be renegades, which means they have no allegiance to anyone but themselves. Normally, I would meet and try to capture them if that is the case, but I cannot take the risk. We must divert and avoid them for your sakes.'

Alice gave a cry of alarm, clinging to her child as the wagon was turned off the road into a field and driven at speed across a surface that was even more rutted and bumpy than the road they had been traversing. Babette turned back and went to reassure her.

'Do not worry, dearest, we shall avoid them. Captain Colby would not allow harm to come to us—and if they should catch up to us he will drive them off.'

'But they could be our friends...' She looked sulky and annoyed at being jostled in such a way.

'They do not wear known colours, which means they are probably renegades. John told you how much trouble they have caused up and down the country, raiding small villages and empty homes.'

Babette frowned as she spoke. Her brother's manor was another day's ride and she could only pray that it had not fallen to one of the renegade bands that were currently roaming the country and robbing villagers and homes.

At the beginning of the war, Babette knew that many people had tried to remain neutral. Her uncle had not been the only one who refused to fight, but over the two years the conflict had spread so that now almost every man was either for the King or Parliament. In all the chaos, as neighbours, cousins and brothers took against each other, sometimes ignoring lifelong friendships, ruthless men seized the chance to make profit for themselves from the misery of others.

She saw that Alice was unconvinced and continued to glance over her shoulder, as though she hoped a troop of Royalists would chase after them and snatch her from the clutches of the Roundheads. Babette bit her lip. Her choice of a husband was bound to split her family, for she doubted that Alice—and perhaps even John—would forgive her. It was a stark choice, but she already knew what she must do. It would break her heart to part from James again. Alice would be safe and cared for at Brevington. She must go with James if he asked her.

There, she had thought of him as James, proof that her choice was made. She would continue to speak of him as Captain Colby to others, but he would be James in her heart and mind.

It had been a long, wearisome journey. Babette sighed with relief when she saw the village of Brevington. Now they had only a few leagues to reach her brother's manor, which lay just beyond the village.

'Thank goodness we are nearly there,' Alice said as she spoke to her. 'I do not know how much more I can bear…jolted through fields and in the company of such men…' A shudder went through her. 'Thank goodness they will soon leave us in peace.'

Alice was so ungrateful and determined in her dislike. Babette had received only politeness and respect at the hands of James's men and she knew it had been the same for Maigret and Alice. The maid had seemed happy enough, even flirting a little with one of the men-at-arms, but Alice had worn a sour expression, grumbling at Babette every chance she got. She was heartily sick of hearing her moan at every inconvenience and had reminded her sharply that they were lucky to have escaped with their lives. To which Alice had countered that, had they waited, they might have travelled with friends.

Babette could hardly restrain her temper, but because she hoped to avoid a breach between them she kept her thoughts to herself. Alice could not be contented to know that she'd been given safe passage to her new home and there was no reasoning with her.

Babette wondered what would happen when they reached the house. Would James leave her with a promise to return as soon as the war was done, or would he take her with him to his home—would he wed her without her brother's consent? She was of an age to marry and surely she could choose for herself and not be dictated to by her brother in this matter?

As they entered the grounds of the manor, Babette caught the stink of smoke or soot. She wrinkled her nose, her heart catching in her breast. There was no sign of smoke in the sky, but... As they came in sight of the house, she felt the pain catch at her breast. John's beautiful house...half of it still stood, but the walls were blackened and the roof had gone. Hearing a wail from Alice, she turned in time to see her scramble down from the cart and go running towards the house. She dismounted and followed her with a sinking heart. Most of the walls still stood, but it would cost a fortune to repair the house—and it could not be attempted until the war was over.

Alice was wailing, screaming and crying. Babette looked at her with pity, but there was little she could say to comfort her. She walked into the ruin to see if anything was left, but what furniture remained was charred beyond recognition. By the look of it, the renegades had taken anything of value before setting the fire.

As she stood undecided, wondering where

they should go next, a servant came running to her.

'Mistress Babs…Mistress Babs…we tried to save the house, but they drove us out and would not let us near until it was well alight. Forgive us. We could do nothing…'

'It is not your fault, Ned,' Babette said. 'Were any of the servants harmed?'

'No, my lady. They said they did not make war on servants, but when we tried to remonstrate they beat us with the flat of their swords and we ran for our lives.'

'Were they Roundheads?'

'Nay, mistress. They looked like Cavaliers in their dress, but they owed allegiance to no one. I told them Lord Harvey was fighting for the King, but they laughed and said they did not care whether he fought for the devil. They came for plunder and burned the house for sport when they had drunk your brother's good wine and malmsey.'

Babette closed her eyes in distress as she saw the scene in her mind. Drunken careless sport that had robbed a man of his home—how could it have come to this? The peaceful England she had known before the war seemed to have been torn apart by this wretched conflict.

'What shall we do?' Alice flew at her, pulling at her sleeve and weeping wildly. 'Where do we go now? You cannot desert me…you would not be so cruel!'

Babette felt as if she were being strangled, torn apart. She could not leave Alice alone when she had no home and no servants to protect her.

'We have some money. We must find lodgings somewhere.'

'I am sorry you find such sorry news here,' James spoke from behind her. 'I can offer you the sanctuary of my house—if you would accept it.'

Babette looked at him, hope in her eyes, but Alice was staring at him in dismay, as if the idea were anathema to her.

'No…' She shook her head. 'I shall not… I cannot.'

'Think before you reject Captain Colby's offer,' Babette said. 'If we have a roof over our heads, we can rest and think. We shall send word to John and he will make arrangements for us to go to him—perhaps in Oxford.'

'We could go on to Oxford,' Alice said, clutching at straws. 'Please, Babette…think of the child and me.'

'I am thinking of you,' Babette said. 'The journey has stretched your nerves to breaking point thus far—to go on to Oxford and perhaps find that John is elsewhere… No, I have made up my mind. I shall accept Captain Colby's offer until John comes to fetch you. You may come with me or go on alone.'

Alice looked mutinous, but she could see that Babette would not be swayed. 'Since you have changed sides it seems that I am at your mercy—a mere prisoner with no power to change your mind. I shall not forgive you for this—and you will be sorry one day.'

'You will not be a prisoner, but a welcome guest,' James assured her, his manner polite in the face of her rudeness. 'You will not long be bothered with my company, Lady Harvey. I shall spend only a few days at my home before leaving to join Cromwell.'

'That monster…' Alice muttered, but was ignored.

'You must leave so soon?' Babette said, her gaze meeting his. 'I had hoped…'

'We shall speak later,' he promised with a warning look. 'When we reach my home. It is but twenty leagues from here and, I promise you, you will be safe there.'

'I know,' she said, and the smile he gave her warmed her heart. 'I am so grateful for all you have done for us, sir.'

'You need never be grateful to me,' he replied, and his eyes caressed her as did the liquid sweetness of his tone. 'You saved my life, mistress. I do not forget. But it is not for that alone that I offer you and your family the hospitality of my home.'

'I understand,' Babette said and she did. He was telling her that he cared for her as a woman—as the woman he wished to marry—and her heart raced with excitement. Perhaps they would be married before he had to leave. 'Thank you.'

Alice glared at her as he moved away. 'I shall send word to Oxford,' she said. 'My letter will be passed to John wherever he is—and I shall leave as soon as he comes to fetch me. If you stay, then you cut yourself off from your family for ever.'

'Please do not be so angry,' Babette said pleadingly. 'I would not be bad friends with my brother's wife. I care for you, the child and John—you know I do.'

'If you cared for me, you would have pressed

on to Oxford,' she said stubbornly, a look of dislike in her eyes.

Babette had never seen her sister-in-law this way and she felt distressed by the change in her. At the castle Alice had seemed grateful for all she did, though sometimes a little selfish. During her pregnancy, when she was often sick and downcast, she clung to Babette, but since the birth some months earlier she had grown more independent and now she was showing the sharpness of her claws for the first time.

Babette turned away, feeling hurt. Alice would have found it hard to travel on so far—and the dangers they faced without Captain Colby's escort might have proved fatal. This house had been attacked within the past few weeks, for the smell of soot was still strong, and the renegades might still be in the area. The gold and jewels Babette carried were all they had left of John's fortune and if that were lost he would have nothing.

'Mistress, may I come with you?' Ned Brewster begged, clutching at her arm. 'I have no other place to live and have been staying here and there, wherever they will give me a bed for a night—and a crust of bread.'

'Yes, of course you may,' Babette said. 'You

may ride on the wagon with Jonas. Are there any more of our people without homes?'

'Nay, mistress. The maids went home—and the young men had gone off to fight, which is why we could not defend ourselves, for it was but I and three women here alone.'

Babette frowned, for it seemed that her brother had left his property undefended. He should have made sure of the loyalty of his men and left at least six stout men-at-arms to defend it. Had he done so, Alice might have had her own home and could have stayed here had she wished.

Babette knew that she no longer felt the need to stay with her and look after her. Alice had made it clear that she was perfectly capable of making her own decisions. She would accompany Babette to Captain Colby's home, because for the moment she had no choice—but as soon as she was able she would leave.

They moved on half an hour later, after they had rested the horses, given them water from the well and eaten food that Ned had purchased from a nearby cottage for them. She saw Alice speaking to a villager and the woman seemed to be offering her something.

Alice seemed to consider for a moment, then shook her head, but then spoke rapidly to the woman, giving her some kind of message—a message for John should he come here, his sister supposed.

She could not blame John's wife for wanting to contact him, but the sullen expression on Alice's face as the little column moved off again made her sad. Why could she not be grateful for the comfort she was offered? There were many in a worse case than they...women and children turned from their homes to fling themselves on the mercy of their relatives. Unfortunately, Babette had no one she could ask for help since her uncle would no longer receive her—and Alice had only a distant aunt whom she had quarrelled with when she ran off with John. The lady had forbidden her to marry without Lord Harvey's consent for she was a woman of stern principles, but Alice had defied her for love and could not now go to her for help.

She had only Babette and her husband to turn to. Knowing that, Babette felt some of her disappointment in Alice abating. Alice was feeling anxious and lonely without her husband. They had lost the castle and now the manor house was useless, because John would find it hard to raise enough money to repair it. Indeed, it was so badly damaged that he might have to tear it down and build new. If the King won the war, he would surely regain his property—and perhaps some reparation for his losses would be made?

She frowned because she knew it would be hard for him, but then it must be hard for hundreds of other men who had given up their homes and livelihoods to fight—on whatever side. Would houses that had been captured ever be returned to their rightful owners? It might take years to do so whatever the outcome of the war—and some men would simply be ruined.

Had John made provision for his family elsewhere? For a moment she wondered if she ought to have let Alice have her way and go on to Oxford, but had they arrived there alone, it would have been difficult to find lodgings they could afford without depleting John's small fortune.

She worried over her brother and his family, but she was not responsible for their future. As yet her own future was not settled, though James intended to make her his wife.

Sighing, she looked at his back, saw the pride and strength in him and smiled.

For the moment she would take what happiness she could.

'What do you think of my home, mistress?' James asked as he came to help her dismount, his hands about her waist. 'Do you think you will be happy here?'

'Yes, from what I have seen,' she said and smiled. They had approached past farms that looked lush with heavy crops and had an air of well-being. The woods were thick and teemed with birds and game, and the orchard was beginning to show signs of the fruit it would bear later that year. 'I like it well.'

The house was large, more impressive than Brevington and fortified with a moat and gatehouse, which her brother's manor had not been. The walls were of a faded yellow stone, the roof of grey slate and the windows long and narrow, set with tiny leaded panes of dull glass. Over one long wall, a pale lilac wisteria had spread outwards and upwards, hiding the stonework, though cleared away from the windows; its scent was heavy on the early summer air. It was a house of three storeys, the win-

dows in the attics protruding outwards in the
form of dormers, square and shapely. There
were pillars along the front and, under a pro-
tecting sloped roof, a long veranda with a balustrade, which was overrun with roses, still
in bud as now. Babette thought they would be
glorious in full summer bloom.

She could not wait to go inside, and when
they did could hardly keep from exclaiming at
the beauty of walls panelled in mellow golden
oak. The floors were of some heavy limestone
tile, but covered here and there with rich carpets and rugs in colours of crimson, gold,
cream and dark blue. Pictures and an occa-
sional mirror hung on the walls, the frames
heavily carved in ornate patterns. The furniture was mainly good English oak, but there
were also a few pieces of walnut, which looked
as if they might be Dutch. A huge court cupboard in the Great Hall was set with pewter
and silver, also bowls of either alabaster or
jade; there were intricate carvings of what she
thought might be soapstone, which she knew
came from far-off China. She saw a beautiful
posset set of Venetian glass and several carved
wooden stands, which held books or needle-

work frames or musical instruments, and everywhere smelled of lavender.

It was a house created with love…for Jane perhaps? Babette felt a stab of pain. He must have loved her very much to gather so many beautiful things here for her sake.

Would he ever love Babette as much?

For a moment the doubts assailed her but when he looked at her, his brows raised, she thrust them from her mind.

'It is a beautiful house, James,' she said from the heart. 'Any woman would be proud to live here.'

'I am glad you like my home. It was my grandfather's house, passed down through my family. I had it refurbished a few years ago when I returned from my travels. I hoped to be happy here.' His voice trailed away as he gazed down at her. 'Shall you be happy here, Babs?'

'Yes, I think so—I know I could be.' She felt the faint tinge of warmth in her cheeks, as his look deepened and she wished that he would take her in his arms and tell her of his love.

Hearing a wailing sound from behind her, she turned to see Alice looking at her balefully. John's son was screaming, clearly wet or hungry, but it was the look of resentment in Alice's eyes that made her shudder. She clearly felt it unfair that Captain Colby's home should be untouched while hers had been destroyed.

'Your son is tired and needs attention,' James said, as a woman came silently to stand close to him. 'Will you take our guests to the chambers I sent word you were to prepare, please? This lady is Mistress Babette—the lady I intend to marry—and Lady Harvey is the wife of Lord Harvey.'

'But she is… They are…' The woman stared at Babette proudly, as if she, too, resented seeing her here. 'Yes, Captain Colby. Do you wish me to take them upstairs?'

'Please.' James reached out for Babette's hands and held them. 'Go with Mrs Brisket, Babs. She has been with my family for years and naturally feels uncertain for the moment— but once she knows you, she will see that you are just the person this house needs.' He spoke in a soft voice that did not carry to the others, but glancing at the housekeeper, Babs knew that it would take some effort on her part to break down the older woman's prejudice. Perhaps she did not like the idea of Royalists in the house—or perhaps there was another reason for her cold reserve.

Babs followed her up the wide wooden staircase, admiring the carving on the balustrade. Everything in this house was to be admired. It was the perfect home for any woman fortunate enough to come here as a bride.

She just hoped that James would stay here long enough to make her his bride. Perhaps when he was ready, he would tell her just what was in his mind.

Chapter Ten

It was more than two hours before Babette received the message that Captain Colby wished to speak with her. Maigret had been sent with the message, and Babette was glad to see that the girl seemed perfectly content with her place.

'Shall you be happy here?' Babette asked her.

'Yes, mistress,' the girl said. 'Mistress Brisket's tongue is sharp, but the steward is called Lewis and he has told me I am welcome here. He says it is time the house had a mistress and will be on your side if the old battleaxe tries to make mischief.'

'You must not call her that, even if she is not as welcoming as we should like.' Babette hid her smile, for the maid did not change and it was her forthright way of speaking that she liked. 'We are guests in this house for the moment.'

'You'll be mistress of it soon enough,' Maigret said with a cheeky look. 'It's plain to see that Captain Colby is in love with you.'

'Yes, perhaps.' Babette smiled, feeling happy as she went down to the small back parlour where James was waiting for her. He turned with a look of welcome on his face and held out his hand to her. She went up to him and took it. Still holding her hand, he went down on one knee in front of her.

'It is my honour to ask you to be my wife, Mistress Babette. You know that I admire and care for you and I would think myself fortunate if you should answer yes.'

'My answer is "yes" with all my heart,' Babette said. 'Please rise, sir.' He did so immediately and swept her into his arms. His mouth was warm and tender as he took possession of hers, gradually deepening his kiss. When her lips parted slightly beneath his kiss, he flicked at them with his tongue, touching hers delicately and tasting her.

'You taste delicious, like honey and wine,' he told her and then released her while he reached inside his doublet and withdrew a ring of heavy gold. It had a small cabochon ruby inset into the gold and, as he slid it on her finger, she felt the snug fit, as if it had been made for her. 'This belonged to my grandmother. I shall have a new ring made for you, Babs, but I wanted you to have something as proof of our betrothal. We are promised to each other, though we have not the benefit of a priest, but it as binding to me as if we were wed.'

'James…it is beautiful, I need no other ring,' she said softly and looked up at him, emotion flowing through her. 'I have longed for this moment, though I did not know if the day would ever come when we should meet again. My brother spoke of wedding me to a friend of his, but I told him I would wait until Alice no longer needed me.'

'You know that as your sister she is welcome to stay here with her child until her husband can come for her…' His eyes seemed to glow with a deep passion and fire as he gazed at her. 'I would that we could be wed before I leave, but the vicar would need papers to prove that you were of an age to marry, unless he had your brother's written consent.'

'I am past the age of needing it, as I would

testify,' she said. Her heart felt full of love for him, her eyes misting with emotion. 'I would be your wife now, James, if it could be done.'

'Are you sure you would not rather wait for Lord Harvey's consent?'

'I fear he would not give it,' she admitted frankly. 'I know that I must choose between my family and you—I choose you.'

He touched her cheek with his fingertips. 'I shall speak to the Reverend Simmons and, if he will perform the ceremony, we shall wed before I leave you.'

'Yes, please,' she said and lifted her face shyly for his kiss. 'We are at war, James, and neither of us knows if we shall meet again or when. If we could have a brief time of happiness as man and wife, it would mean so much to me.'

'And to me,' he agreed. 'I thought only of you, but I will speak to Reverend Simmons and do my best to get him to agree to our wedding at such short notice. He may come here and perform the ceremony in the chapel. My servants will witness it and your sister-in-law, too, if she wishes.'

'She may refuse, for she thinks I have betrayed her by coming here,' Babette said. 'But

I do not care for anything but that we are together once more.'

'I swear you are more beautiful and precious than I deserve,' he said and kissed her again, so tenderly that it drew the heart from her body and made her cling to him. 'I am the most fortunate of men to have found you.'

'I, too, am fortunate,' she said and her stomach clenched with something she dimly recognised as sweet desire. Her lips felt full and parted as she breathed deeply, betraying her need and the hot wanting within. 'When we met I thought you arrogant and my enemy, but now I know how wrong I was.'

James smiled and caressed the side of her cheek with his hand, seeing the smoky passion in her eyes and knowing that she had answered his need with an equal desire of her own. How real and true a woman she was. Not a gentle child, as Jane had been, but a woman with needs and desires. She could match him and he could let his passion have free rein without fear of frightening her. At that moment his longing to make her his own in truth was almost overwhelming. Only his care for her prevented him from snatching her up and taking her somewhere they could be alone.

'I adore you, my sweet Babs. I shall leave you to settle in now, my love—but I hope to return with the news that we both desire.' He let her go reluctantly, knowing that he must see her safely wed before he indulged his need of her love. In war, anything might happen and he would not have her bear a child out of wedlock, for she would be shunned by everyone and named a wanton.

He walked away, leaving Babette to stand and dream until a sharp voice addressed her and she turned to see the housekeeper looking at her with dislike.

'Lady Harvey wished to speak to you, mistress,' she said, her hostility plain. 'I think the child is unwell, for it will not stop screaming.'

'I dare say the journey has upset poor Jonny,' she said. 'He is usually the sweetest of babies and hardly cries, but I think his napkin has been wet too often. I dare say you might know a recipe for soothing a baby's bottom?'

'Well…' The housekeeper looked thoughtful. 'I might—if you thought it could be of help.'

'I am sure you have something on your shelves, Mistress Brisket—and we are so weary after the journey we should be grateful for your help. My father did not employ a housekeeper and it is such a help to have a wiser head when children are ill. I often felt the lack at the castle.'

Babette saw that her words had softened the older woman's attitude a little. She promised to look in the still room and see what could be found to ease Jonny's sore bottom. Babette had guessed right and it was possibly a fear of losing her place now that there were two women in the house that had made her hostile. Rather than turning her off, Babette would be pleased with her company, for she had much to learn before she could run this house as well as it was already being run. Perhaps if she could convince Mistress Brisket of it she could win her as a friend rather than having her as an enemy.

Babette had guessed right. Jonny's bottom was covered with red patches and clearly very sore. His relief once the healing balm was spread on his tender skin was obvious and, after a feed, he stopped screaming and whimpered until he fell asleep.

Alice's chamber was large, and the housekeeper had supplied a cradle for the child, also blankets and sheets. She returned with an armful of clean napkins and baby gowns, which she said had belonged to Master James when he was a babe.

Babette stayed with her sister-in-law until the child was settled and Alice had been persuaded to sleep. She was exhausted and perhaps her ill temper had stemmed from fear and tiredness.

Going back down the stairs, intending to speak to the housekeeper about the matter of clean clothes for her and Alice, she passed the parlour where she had spoken to James earlier; the door was ajar and she could clearly hear raised voices coming from inside.

'That witch is not worthy to take her place,' a man's voice said furiously. 'I do not know how you could think of bringing her here when this house was meant for my sweet sister.'

'Damn you, sir,' James said, sounding equally angry. 'I do not slight Jane by bringing the woman I intend to wed to my home. You accuse me of forgetting her, but that is a lie. I shall never forget the love we shared, nor cease to mourn for her—but I cannot live alone for ever. I need a chance of happiness—

a warm pair of arms to hold me at night and a mother for the children I hope to have.'

Babette flinched as she listened. Was that all she meant to James—just a warm body to cling to and a mother for his children? Tears stung her eyes, but she held them back. Surely she had always known somewhere at the back of her mind that James still loved his first sweetheart, but in many marriages affection and respect were more than a transient love that passed away after a few months. Yes, it hurt to know that he still loved Jane, but she could bear it—she would love him and hope that he gave her affection as well as passion. Of his physical need she was not in doubt, for it had been in his kiss as well as his eyes.

About to pass on, she heard James curse and cry out in alarm. 'No, man, do not be a fool!' Hearing the ring of metal strike something, she gasped and pushed open the door, staring at the terrifying scene that met her gaze. The man she knew to be Jane's brother had drawn a sword and seemed to be on the verge of attacking James. He did not wear a sword in the house and could not defend himself from this unworthy attack.

Looking for a weapon, she saw the metal

fire-iron in the hearth and dashed towards it. Seizing it, she rushed at the stranger's back and brought her weapon down hard on his sword-bearing shoulder. He gave a yelp of pain, cursing as he swung round to meet her attack and thrusting his sword at her. Babette was not quick enough to avoid the thrust and it caught her a glancing blow across her forearm. Even as the blade drew blood, James gave a cry of rage and jumped at the rogue swordsman, grappling him from behind. One arm about his throat, he brought him tumbling down and in another he had stamped on his hand, forcing him to let go of the blade. He kicked it fiercely, sending it skittering across the room to where three male servants had gathered. They had heard the screams and come rushing to assist. One of them retrieved the sword and held it ready.

'Shall I kill him, Captain Colby?' the man asked, growling in his throat. 'That devil tried to murder you—and the lady.'

'Mistress Babette saved my life once more,' James said. His eyes glinted like steel as he stared at the would-be assassin.

'I think this is the second time you have tried to kill me,' he said. 'You may be Jane's brother, but she would be ashamed of you. She was a sweet, gentle girl and she would be deeply hurt that you tried to murder someone she cared for—and that you should harm a woman…'

'You drove Jane to her grave. She was nervous of marriage and you pressed her to marry. She loved you and so agreed, but it made her ill with worry,' Melchet babbled as they dragged him away. 'She was sitting in the rain weeping for hours two days before the wedding, and that's why she took that chill. You murdered her and I loved her. I wanted her to remain pure and untouched. I made her promise…'

The rest of his feverish babbling was lost as the servants dragged him away, still shouting abuse until he could no longer be heard.

Seeing that Babette was bleeding profusely, James took the white linen stock from about his neck and came to her, wrapping it about her arm tightly.

'Someone call Mrs Brisket—and fetch the physician to Mistress Babette.'

Feeling faint, but determined not to give way, Babette clung to his arm. 'Mistress Brisket will bind me and apply her salves. There is no need to send for a...' Giving a little moan, she fainted into James's arms.

Babette knew nothing more until she woke in a bed that smelled of clean linen and lavender some time later.

Mistress Brisket was standing by the bed. She had been applying a cloth soaked in cool water to Babette's forehead and she smiled down at her.

'I told the master you would wake soon,' she said. 'You've slept the night through. The tisane I gave you has eased you, though I think you do not recall it, for you were very faint and hardly knew when I bound your arm.'

'Indeed, I knew nothing of it,' Babette said and pushed herself up against the pile of pillows. 'Forgive me for being such a nuisance, Mistress Brisket. I have caused you a deal of trouble.'

'Nothing is too much trouble for the lady who saved my master from almost certain death. I will confess that I did resent you taking Miss Jane's place, for a sweeter creature never drew breath—but she would have been horrified to see what her brother did. And besides, my master needs a wife and children, as all men do.'

'Yes…' Babette smiled at her weakly. 'How lucky I am that you have skill in the healing arts. I fear I have lost a deal of blood, for I feel weak from it.'

'Yes, it is likely you will for a day or so, though I will bring you some good broth that may give you strength.'

Babette thanked her again and she went away. As the events of the previous evening played through her mind, Babette wondered what had happened after she fainted. What had they done with Jane Melchet's brother? And where was James? He had promised they would marry before he left…but Babette was not certain she had the strength to stand, let alone be married.

She lay back against the pillows, fighting the desire to weep, and then the door opened and someone entered her room. She opened her eyes and saw that James was standing by the bed, looking at her anxiously. He had picked a delicate lily from the garden and, as she smiled at him, presented it to her.

'Thank God you have no fever,' he said. 'I thought…I feared…' His voice caught with emotion, and she knew that he had feared she might die, as Jane had.

'I have no fever,' Babette said and smiled at him, for he certainly cared for her, even if she was not the love of his life. 'It was a glancing stroke, though it bled mightily. I am a little weak, but I shall manage to get up for our wedding—if you have managed to arrange it before you leave?'

'Reverend Simmons thought it best to read the banns in church. I have decided to stay until Sunday to hear the first reading and then I will report to headquarters, but I shall ask permission to take some leave and we shall be married on my return.' He saw the protest in her eyes and smiled tenderly. 'I know you would force yourself to leave your bed if I would let you, dearest Babs, but I prefer that you rest. If you are strong enough, we will hear the banns read together, if not, I will hear them alone. It will be no more than two or three weeks at the most before I return to you.'

Babette held her sigh inside. She gave him her hand as he sat on the edge of the bed and then leaned down to kiss her. His kiss was gentle and without passion, but she longed for more. How immodest she was! If James could wait for their wedding, then so must she. It would be unseemly to insist on a hasty wedding since he seemed content to wait and would alter his plans to return to her.

'It shall be as you desire,' she said meekly and saw the light of laughter in his eyes.

'Oh, how hard that was for you to say,' he mocked her gently. 'I know you for the bold, brave wench you are, Babette, and would have you no different—but in this case I think it best to wait a little. I should be a brute to insist on my wedding night when my bride was injured in the most foolish and yet bravest action I have seen in a lady.'

Babette's throat felt tight. The way he looked at her now she could almost believe that she was the most precious thing in his life—but she knew that no one could replace his sweet Jane. She was not his first love, but perhaps she would be his last. He would come to love her, because she would be all that he could ever desire in a wife.

'What happened to—?' she began tentatively, but he anticipated her.

'Herbert Melchet has gone,' James said. 'He has been warned that if he dares to venture on to my land again he will be shot like the mad dog he is. For some reason he blames me for his sister's death, though God knows I would never have harmed her. He claimed that I pushed her into marriage, but it is a lie. She named the day.'

'I think that perhaps he was jealous of her love for you. He must be truly out of his mind,' Babette said, looking at him anxiously. 'To try to kill you in your own parlour...'

'I had only to raise my voice and the men would have come,' James said, frowning at her. 'Promise me you will not do anything so foolish again. I could have defended myself with a chair had I chosen, but I was shocked that he should attack me when he had been my friend. I hoped to talk to him, to make him see sense and put away his sword and make an end to this feud—but it will not happen now. He attacked you and I shall never call him friend again.'

Babette remained silent. She believed that only her swift action had saved him. No doubt James would have found some kind of a weapon had she not struck first, but Melchet had been out for blood, and James had had no sword. She was not sure that he could have fought off a man determined on murder, but

she would not argue for it was not seemly in a
woman to argue in such a case.

'I promise only to restrain myself until I see
that action is necessary,' she said and smiled
up at him. 'Mrs Brisket is to make me some
broth and I think that will restore me—enough
to hear the banns read on Sunday.'

At least she would have two more days more
before he left her to return to his unit. She
prayed fervently that it would not be more than
three weeks before he returned to wed her.

'I have come to apologise,' Alice said as
she crept a little shame-faced into the room
the next morning. 'I said some unforgivable
things to you on the way here and I am sorry.'

'You were tired and anxious,' Babette said.
'There is nothing to forgive, Alice. I hope we
shall continue to be friends—even though I
know you do not wish to be here.'

'No, I do not wish it, though I admit it is a
comfortable home and I envy you your future
life, Babs. Captain Colby is a gentleman—and
wealthy, I think. I do not know how we shall
go on. John has lost everything in the King's
cause.'

'Perhaps not quite all,' Babette said. 'We

managed to save your jewels and a little gold. It is enough to set you up in a small house until John can find some way of restoring his fortunes. If the King wins the war, the castle will be his again—and perhaps reparation will be made for Brevington.'

'Perhaps…' she said, a sullen look creeping back into her eyes. 'But what if the King does not win?'

'You must not doubt it,' Babette said, though in her heart she believed that it might happen. From what she'd seen at the castle she believed the men Cromwell had trained were more determined than many Royalists. 'As soon as John gets your letter he will make arrangements for you to join him somewhere.'

Alice nodded, but did not look happy. Having begun by apologising, she went on to complain about almost everything: she did not have enough clothes, many of her trinkets had been left behind and she did not like having to sit at table with men who were her husband's enemies.

Babette listened and soothed her as best she could, agreeing that they would spend a little of John's gold by buying cloth in the market as soon as they were able. However, there was no contenting her and she went away as sullen as before.

Babette sighed, because her head had begun to ache. She was glad when Mrs Brisket entered with a tray bearing a bowl of good oxtail soup and some fresh bread and butter. She set the tray over Babette's knees and was about to depart when Babette asked where the nearest cloth merchant resided.

'Is there a market where we could buy clothes? Most of ours were left behind when we fled the castle…'

'I dare say there are trunks in the attics… cloth and whole garments. The clothes would need alteration, for they belonged to the old mistress, but I am certain the master would permit you to use them.'

Babette thanked her and ate her broth. It was tasty and warming and she felt better as the food filled her stomach. She had not eaten food like this for some days and felt glad to be somewhere she could be at ease. Her hands stroked over the silken coverlets and the soft fresh linen. How much luckier she was than Alice. It was no wonder that her sister-in-law was out of sorts, for she had lost two homes in as many weeks. Babette had come home and felt the surge of pleasure as she contemplated living here for the rest of her life.

How lucky she was to have found James.

Babette was able to get up that afternoon. She walked a little shakily to the window and looked down at the courtyard garden; it was much as she had tended at her aunt's house, filled with flowers, herbs and the hives that would give them a wealth of the rich honey that was so important to all their lives.

'Are you certain you should be out of bed?'

At the sound of James's voice, she swung round, grabbing at the back of a chair for support. She was still a little unsteady, but better than she had been and she smiled at him.

'I shall be able to accompany you to church to hear the banns read,' she said. 'I am getting stronger all the time.'

'Mrs Brisket has made me aware of your lack,' he said. 'You are, of course, free to make use of any clothes or materials in the attics, but I shall order cloth for you from London—and a gown for your wedding. A seamstress will be fetched to make up the silk for you.'

'I can make it myself if I have the material,'

she said. 'I like to sew and it is something I do well.'

'Then you may find much of what you need in my mother's trunks,' James said. 'However, my wife shall have whatever she needs in the way of finery. I have money enough for all the little pleasures of life and you have only to ask for whatever you need.'

'Alice is also in need of clothes,' Babette said. 'I am certain we can find garments that may be altered for us both—and if there is cloth we shall make new ones.'

It would be something to do in the long days and nights when he was gone from her. Even though he had promised to return and wed her, she knew that the visit would be brief. He would leave her again and again over the months to come, because there was a war he was determined must be won.

Babette sat beside James in the church as the vicar gave his sermon and then read out the announcement of their wedding. She knew that she looked pale and she still felt a little weak, but she had been determined to be here for the first reading. Holding James's hand, she smiled as she felt the pressure of his fingers. He turned his head to look at her, his eyes caressing as they moved over her face.

'Are you tired, dear heart?'

'A little,' she replied, 'but I am gaining strength daily. I shall be well again when you return.'

'Yes, I am sure of it,' he said and held her hand so tightly that it was almost painful.

Afterwards, he held her arm so that she leaned on him as they walked from church. Outside in the sunshine, his friends and neighbours came to greet him and smile on her, welcoming her to their midst and promising to call on her. James invited them all to the wedding and a reception at his home afterwards, saying that the date was not set, but they would all be welcome when it happened.

'I think you will have friends to make now,' he said. 'My neighbours are kindly folk and they will take you to their hearts. I am sure that the way you fought for me will have been heard in every house by now. I saw the admiring glances my friends gave you and I shall be envied by every man in the district.'

'No, surely not,' Babette laughed, enjoying his teasing. 'I saw some very pretty young ladies in church…'

Chapter Eleven

Babette stood and watched her affianced husband ride away later that afternoon. He had left five of his men at the manor, added to the ten who had always remained to guard his property. There were three women servants besides Maigret who had come with Babette, the steward and a score of men who worked either in the gardens, the kitchens or the various workshops that supplied the house. With Mrs Brisket, Maigret and the other servants Babette would be well served and cared for and she had her sister-in-law as her companion, but she felt bereft, as if cast out alone.

She was so foolish! Babette shut away the tears that pressed against her eyes and the feeling of despair that swept over her. James had his duty and like any man must attend his affairs, and she had a new home to order as she wished.

'This house is your home, Babs,' James had told her, holding her hands as they took leave of each other in private. 'You must have things as you wish. Mrs Brisket has run it well enough in the absence of a mistress, but you are to be my wife and if there is anything you wish to change you must do so.'

'Yes, of course, in little ways and gradually,' she replied and smiled. 'Mrs Brisket is a good housekeeper, James. We shall discuss what food is ordered and served and I may make suggestions. As for the linen and stores… well, as a good wife I must make lists and see what may be improved.'

'I can see you need no advice from me,' James said and bent to kiss her softly on the lips. A sound of regret left his lips as he drew away, and he looked rueful. 'How I wish that I might stay here for ever at your side, but my duty calls.'

'Yes, I know,' she said and kept her sigh inside for he must take the memory of her smile with him; to cling and weep would only make the parting harder. 'Go, James. Your duty is clear. When you return we shall be wed and then…' She shook her head, because she knew that life was uncertain for perhaps years to come.

'You will be all right here?'

'Yes, of course,' Babette said. 'Your people are loyal to you and will protect me as your wife-to-be. Go with an easy mind, James. I shall be waiting and ready to be your wife when you return.'

And so he had ridden away, leaving her feeling bereft, but she must not let her unease show. Alice refused to be comforted and continued to grumble, despite the comfort and attentions that had been paid her. She might have been content here at Colby had she wished, but her face wore a permanent look of dissatisfaction.

As the little column disappeared from her sight, Babette went inside the house. Mrs Brisket had set the maidservants to polishing and the scent of lavender and beeswax met her as she walked into the small parlour she had come to think of as her own. Alice was already there with a piece of embroidery. She looked up as Babette entered.

'Have they gone?'

'Yes. James promised to pass your letter on.

A courier will be dispatched to Oxford. If John is there, it should find him, but it may be some weeks before he can come for you.'

'You will be married before then—if Captain Colby returns for you.'

'James will return as soon as he is able,' Babette said, struggling to keep the impatience from her voice. She did not need reminding that James could be wounded or killed. She had lived with the knowledge for the past year or more and her joy at having seen him, held him and kissed him would sustain her in the next few weeks. Despite Alice, she would not let herself think of the alternative.

James would not die. He would return to claim her as he had promised.

'It is more than six months since John came back to me,' Alice replied, a look of such misery in her eyes that Babette was touched. 'I think he is dead. I think he is dead and I shall never see him again. I am alone with my son…I have no home…'

Babette knew that she was waiting for her to reassure her, but she refused to be drawn down that road. 'John will come as soon as he can,' she said. 'Had he been killed someone would have come to the castle to tell us.'

Alice sniffed and blew her nose on her handkerchief. She did not answer, but bent her head over her needlework, the picture of dejection.

Babette left her to her work. She had decided that she would talk to Mrs Brisket about what was needed for their stores and whether an inventory of the linen had been taken in the spring.

Ten days passed pleasantly enough. Babette kept busy and refused to allow Alice's grumbles and dark hints to disturb her. She joined her housekeeper in the kitchen each morning, and they discussed the tasks for the servants, menus and the various stores needed. Babette sometimes showed her maids how she liked a certain dish made, but she did not cook meals or perform menial chores, for James expected his wife to be a lady and the chaperon of his home. On warm afternoons she walked in her gardens, discussing the planting with the gardeners and making sure that they were growing the herbs and flowers she needed for her cures. She had begun to make one or two of her own cures and spent some happy hours discussing the recipes with Mrs Brisket, who was also very knowledgeable in such matters and did not imagine that her mistress was a witch for knowing them.

After their first hostile meeting, the house-keeper had unbent more and more and was now devoted to her new mistress and the child. She fussed over the baby, changing his nappy when he cried and giving him more attention than his mother ever had. Although she did not say so, Babette knew that Mrs Brisket did not approve of Alice very much, but the words remained unspoken.

It was on the afternoon of the tenth day that one of the servants came into the garden to look for Babette and tell her that a visitor had arrived.

'He wishes to speak to you—and says he has a message for you, mistress, but I think… he seems suspicious to me.'

'Thank you, Tom,' Babette said, and her heart caught with anxiety. Who could the messenger be—and why had he aroused her servant's suspicion?

Babette pulled off the gloves she'd worn to protect her hands, thrusting them into the basket that carried the herbs she had been gathering. She set the basket down in the hall and hurried through to the parlour. A man was standing before the window, his back towards her; his dress proclaimed him a Royalist and she understood her servant's suspicion, for to him he represented the enemy. However, Babette knew him at once.

'Drew Melbourne,' she said. 'What brings you here?'

He turned to face her, and as she saw his expression, a shiver went through her. She reached for the back of a chair, holding on to it as her head began to whirl and her heart raced.

'Forgive me,' Drew said. 'I am the bearer of ill news and I wish I had not been...but I must tell you that John was wounded and lies ill at Oxford. I am not sure that he will survive long enough for you to reach him, but he begs that you will come.'

'Surely it is Alice he needs,' Babette said. All her senses were protesting, for she did not wish to leave the home she was coming to love. What would James think if she were not here when he returned? He would believe that she had deserted him. 'I am to be wed soon—to your cousin, sir.'

'Yes, I am aware of this,' Drew replied. 'James Colby forwarded Alice's letter to us, as he promised you. However, Alice has little skill in nursing and I do not forget that you saved my life. I fear that John may die unless you come to him.'

'I am sorry for my brother's situation,' Babette said, her chest tight with emotion, 'of course I am, but I do not wish to leave here. You have no right to ask it of me.'

'James will understand that you had to go to your brother. I know him for a decent, God-fearing man. In God's mercy, lady, you cannot deny your brother when he needs you.' His dark eyes accused her and she could not meet them, for he was right.

Babette's throat was tight. She cared for her brother, but she was afraid that if she went to him in Oxford and he recovered, he would try to detain her there. He would not wish her to leave and return to James—and how would she make the long journey alone? Yet how could she desert her brother when he needed her? To do so would be a shameful act and lie heavy on her conscience. If he should die…

'I know it is unfair,' Drew said. 'I will give my word that I will escort you back here when John has recovered—will that content you?'

Babette's eyes stung with tears. She was

being torn apart and it was unfair, but in her heart she knew she could not refuse his request.

'Why did you not ask for Alice?'

'You know she will scream and weep. I beg you to comfort her, Mistress Babette. You are so much stronger than she and she will need you in the days ahead.'

It was true. Alice would be little use at nursing her husband and, if he should die, she would be grief-stricken. Babette had no choice but to go with them.

'I must leave a letter for James,' she said reluctantly. 'I will tell Alice for you and we will be ready to leave in an hour.'

'Thank you.' He smiled approvingly. 'I knew that I might place my trust in you.'

'You promise that you will return me to my home?'

'I give you my word.'

'Then I shall leave you, for there is much to do.'

Babette left him and made her way to Alice's chamber. She was nursing the child and for once looked happy. Babette's heart sank because she did not relish the task of telling her sister-in-law that her husband was very ill.

'What is it?' Alice was suddenly still, seeming to sense her mood. 'Something has happened…it is John. Is he dead?'

'Wounded. He needs our help, Alice. I have promised to accompany you to Oxford and help you to nurse him…and then I shall return here with Drew Melbourne's escort.'

'You are coming to Oxford with us?' Alice stared at her, her eyes wide and frightened. 'He is dying, isn't he? I have known for days that something was wrong.'

Perhaps she had. Sometimes it was possible to know these things without being told. Babette felt guilty for having misjudged her, thinking her moods merely selfish.

'Drew asked me to help with the nursing. I have given my word. Pack what you need, Alice. I must write a letter to James and then I shall gather my things. I told Drew we should leave in an hour.'

'Then I must hurry,' Alice said. 'Thank you, Babette. I do not think I could face this alone.'

Babette was surprised at how calm Alice seemed. It was almost as though she had expected the worst and now that it had happened she was calm, even relieved.

Leaving her to pack her clothes, Babette

went to her own chamber. She sat at her table and, dipping her quill in the inkpot, she wrote her letter to James. It was filled with her regret and her hopes that she would return in time for their wedding. She begged him for his under-standing, explaining that she could not desert Alice and her brother at such a time. Her throat tight with tears, she sealed the paper with hot wax and took it downstairs.

Calling Mrs Brisket to her in her parlour, she gave her the letter and told her that she had been summoned to her brother's bedside.

'He is very ill and may die before I reach Oxford,' she said. 'I do not wish to leave, but I cannot desert my family at such a time. I shall return the moment I am able.'

'I shall give your letter to the master,' Mrs Brisket said. She placed the sealed paper on the mantelpiece, behind the large silver cande-labra. 'I shall draw his attention to your mes-sage, my lady—and if you return before he does you will find it there.'

'Thank you.' Babette sighed. 'I am so sorry to leave.'

'It is a sad thing for you and we shall miss you, but it is your duty to go. Will you take your servants with you?'

'I think Maigret and Jonas must accompany

us, but Ned can remain here. He is useful in the fields and has settled well. I shall not uproot him. Besides, I hope to return before Captain Colby comes home.'

Bidding her farewell, Babette went upstairs to finish her packing, and Mrs Brisket to the kitchen. Neither of them witnessed Alice as she entered the room in search of her needle-work, nor did they see what she did there.

Half an hour later the small cavalcade moved off. Drew had brought riding horses for the ladies and Jonas drove the wagon with Maigret sitting beside him and the baby lying in a bed of cushions and blankets in the back of the wagon.

Alice seemed much more cheerful than she had for weeks. Babette had begun to worry for her brother, wondering if they would reach him in time, and was a little surprised to hear her sister-in-law laugh at some remark of Drew's. She looked at him in a way that Babette felt was almost flirtatious, fluttering her lashes and pouting at him. Indeed, she seemed to have thrown off the sullen mood of the past few months, more lively and excited than Babette had ever seen her.

* * *

'Are you all right, Alice?' she asked when they stopped for some food.

'Yes, why not?' Alice said. 'We shall be in Oxford and at last I shall have people to talk to rather than being cooped up in that awful castle. John told me that we should live in the manor house, but he broke his word to me. At least now I shall have some freedom…and I shall not have to live in a rebel's house.'

Babette felt hurt that she could speak so coldly of the kindness and hospitality that she had received in James's house. She felt uncertain of Alice, surprised at her manner and the careless mood that had come over her. She had expected tears or even hysterics, but Alice was cool and even a little excited to be travelling to Oxford. She asked Drew endless questions about it, the King and his court, as if she were going for a pleasant visit rather than to the bedside of her sick husband.

More than that, she treated Babette with disdain. Sometimes she looked at her with an expression akin to hatred or acute dislike. Why had she turned against her? Was it just that Babette had refused to go to Oxford in the first place, forcing Alice to accompany her to

James's home? What was even more disturb-
ing was that she refused to allow Babette to
nurse her son, preferring that Maigret should
take him when he cried. At the castle and on
their flight from it, Alice had clung to Babette,
but now she had turned against her.

The coldness seemed to grow stronger as
they travelled and, by the time they approached
Oxford, Alice seldom spoke more than two
words together to Babette. Hurt by her attitude
and then angered by her proud, cold manner,
Babette withdrew from her and stopped offering to help her.

She had never been to Oxford before and
was interested as they rode in to see how many
church spires there were. The town was ancient
and rather beautiful, also very busy, a market
in progress as they made their way through the
streets to a house of decent proportions close
to the Cathedral. It was plain to see that this
city was a Royalist stronghold, for it was well
defended and men in hats with large plumes
and brightly coloured clothes paraded through
the town. Several of them noticed the ladies
and swept off their hats, bowing and smiling as
they rode by. Once, Babette thought she caught

sight of Captain Richards, but she could not be sure, for he was riding through the street that crossed theirs and she could not be certain.

As they stopped outside the house, a rather pretty young woman looked out and beckoned to them in relief.

'You must be Mistress Babette,' she said. 'Will you go up to your brother at once, please? The first chamber at the top of the stairs. Lord Harvey is very ill and he has asked for you several times.'

Alice gave a little cry and ran past Babette, thrusting her aside as she rushed upstairs. As Babette followed a little more slowly, she heard a fearful scream. Alice came to the head of the stairs and now the tears she had held back earlier were streaming down her cheeks.

'He is dying,' she said. 'You must save him… you must. You owe it to me.'

Babette ignored her and went into the room she had left. Going towards the bed, she saw that the man in the bed looked a strange yellow colour, his eyes sunken and his skin had a waxen look. He was staring at her feverishly, but he did not know her. She placed a hand on his brow. He was burning up, so hot that she could not wonder he tossed and threw his limbs from side to side.

'May I help you?' the woman who had greeted them asked in a soft voice. 'I am Beth. Drew asked me to do what I could for your brother, mistress, but I am not skilled in the arts of nursing. He called for you at first, but these past two days he has hardly spoken, though I think it was your name he called.'

'He loves his wife very much, but he knows I have some skill in healing,' Babette said. 'If you could bring me a bowl of cool water and a towel, please? I must bathe him to reduce this heat, for he cannot bear it—and then when he is a little easier I shall make a tisane that will help the fever.'

'Yes, of course. I can help you turn him— and then I must leave you until the morning. My father expects me home. He does not know that I have been caring for Drew's friend. He would not think it proper.'

'Are you not yet married?'

'I wish that we were,' Beth said and sighed. 'My parents forbid it. They say that Drew leads too dangerous a life and they would not see me a widow before I am a wife—and I am but seventeen. Had there been no war I might have been wed this year.' Her cheeks flushed. 'We fell in love when I was but fourteen, but my father said we must wait until I was seventeen. It has been a long wait and now Father says I must wait until the war is over...'

'Then you have my sympathy,' Babette said. 'It seems hardly fair that you should have to wait now that you are old enough to wed.'

Babette had pulled off the heavy covers, leaving only the sheet to cover John's modesty.

'Perhaps you should fetch the water and then leave me to manage,' she suggested. 'Your mother would not think it fitting that you should see a man naked, and John must be so if I am to bathe him.'

'Then I shall bring the water and leave,' Beth said, a faint flush in her cheeks.

Babette bent over her brother once more, stroking the damp hair back from his forehead. 'Alice is here,' she said. 'She will come to sit with you when you are a little better. You must fight, my dear. I can help you—but not if you give up.'

John threw out his arm and groaned. She thought he seemed slightly easier, turning with a smile as Beth brought the water.

'Thank you. I can manage now. It was good of you to come.'

'He is Drew's friend and saved his life… with your help. I wish that I could have done more. I fetched the physician, but he was not a great deal of help, though he dressed his wound a few times.'

Not often enough, Babette thought as she looked at the stained dressing. As Beth left the room, she was beginning to bathe her brother's heated body. When he was easier she would remove that bloody bandage and rebind him with some healing salve, which she had brought with her.

It was only when she went downstairs with the bowl and dirty linen that she saw Alice speaking with a woman who was clearly the housekeeper. They both looked at her and she thought she saw a hint of hostility in both pairs of eyes. What had Alice been saying behind her back?

'John is a little better now that he has been cooled,' she said. 'His wound looks to be healing, but it is the fever that is dangerous. I need to brew him a tisane from the herbs I brought with me. May I have some hot water, please?'

The housekeeper looked at Alice, who nodded.

'If you would follow me, Mistress Harvey,'

she said. 'I shall show you where the kitchen is—and your things have been taken to the attic.'

'The attic?' Babette stared at her. 'I would prefer one of the guestrooms, if you do not mind—I fear I do not know your name, mistress?'

'I am Mistress Jones,' the woman said sourly. 'There are only three guestrooms. Captain Melbourne has one, Lord Harvey the second—and Lady Harvey and her son the third. The only room left for you is in the attic with the…servant you brought with you.'

Babette bit back the angry words that rose to her lips. So she was to be treated as a servant in her brother's house, was she? Well, she would not stay here a moment longer than need be. She had come here against her wishes to do what she could for John and now she was to be treated as a stranger.

Alice must hate her very much to have done this to her. She could at least have shared her room with Babette until John was well enough for her to share his bed.

Swallowing her anger behind a proud face, Babette accepted the situation. She would leave this house the moment she could.

* * *

'I do not understand,' James said, looking at his housekeeper in dismay. 'Why would she go? She knew that I meant to return as soon as I was able. We are to be wed in a few days.'

'I think it was Captain Melbourne who came to fetch her.'

'My cousin?' James frowned. 'I did not know she was acquainted with him…where did they go?'

'To Oxford, I think.' Mrs Brisket frowned. 'I understood her brother was lying close to death and…she gave me a letter for you, sir. I placed it on the mantelpiece in the small parlour, but after they left I saw it had gone.'

'Are you saying she chose not to leave it?'

'I do not know, Captain. Mistress Babette seemed most distressed to be leaving. Indeed, I would swear she did not want to go.' Her brow creased in a frown. 'I do not know if I should say…but it struck me that her sister-in-law was unpleasant to her at times.'

'Was she indeed?'

James was thoughtful as he went into the small parlour. He searched for the letter lest it should have fallen down somewhere, but there was no sign of it. Why would Babette have changed her mind? If she had gone to the trouble to write to him and left it with Mrs Brisket, it was unlikely that she would decide to tear it up—why would she do that? If she'd wanted to tell him she no longer wished to be his wife, she would have certainly left the letter for him…and yet Mrs Brisket seemed certain that she had intended to come back.

He had been lucky enough to return sooner than he'd hoped, his desire to make Babette his wife so strong that he had taken an extended leave against Cromwell's wishes. His decision not to join him on his next excursion had not pleased his leader, but James had decided that Babette must come first—and now she had gone with no word for him.

What could have happened to her letter? Babette was not in the habit of changing her mind once she had decided what she must do. If she considered it her duty, she might not have gone willingly and would certainly have wanted him to understand—so where had the letter gone?

Had someone taken it? He immediately dismissed his own people, for they had no reason to cause her grief. If what Mrs Brisket had said was true, the one person who might wish to hurt her was her brother's wife.

He had known that Lady Harvey did not wish to come here. He had witnessed the argument when she had tried to push her sister-in-law into going to Oxford with her. Now it seemed she had had her way. Had she stolen the letter to cause trouble between them, hoping that he would simply allow Babette to leave him?

If Lady Harvey imagined that he would abandon Babette so easily she did not know him. He recalled that Babette had told him that her brother had wished to push her into a marriage with one of his friends—was this a trick to lure her back to Oxford and prevent their marriage?

There was only one way to discover the truth. He must go to Oxford in search of the woman he loved. If Babette no longer wished to wed him, she would tell him to his face—and if she were being kept there against her will… Well, then he would bring her home with him.

Chapter Twelve

Babette pressed a hand to the bottom of her back, smothering a sigh. She had been sitting with her brother for most of the day and night for nearly six days. It was the only place in the house where she felt needed or wanted. Alice would hardly look at her and never spoke to her if she could avoid it. Even her daily report on John's recovery was listened to with a distant air, as if Alice did not wish to know. She had visited her husband only a few times and would not sit with him.

'You are here to nurse him,' she said. 'It is your duty as his sister. You have lived under our roof for too long, now you can earn your keep.'

Babette refused to answer her. She did not know what Alice did with her days. She had

demanded her jewels and John's gold as soon
as they had left James's house under Drew
Melbourne's escort and Babette had given
them to her, reserving nothing for herself—
something she now regretted since she had
seen her sister-in-law wearing at least three
new silk gowns. She herself had only the two
gowns she had brought with her and she could
not afford to buy anything for herself.

Hearing laughter from outside the house,
she rose and walked over to the window to
glance out. What she saw on the pavement
below made her frown, for Alice was walking arm in arm with a Cavalier and she knew
him for Captain Richards. As she watched,
Alice glanced up and saw her, a scowl passing
across her pretty face. She said something to
her companion, who replied without glancing
up; his reply made Alice laugh and they went
into the house together. She turned away from
the window, pressing a hand to her back once
more and suppressing a sigh.

'How long have you been here, Babs?'
John's voice was faint but clear, and Babette
felt a surge of pleasure as she looked at the bed
and saw that he was watching her. 'I have been
very ill, I think?'

'Very,' Babette confirmed as she hastened to the bed, slipping her arm about him to help ease him up against the pillows. 'Do not try to do too much just yet. You are bound to be very weak.'

John nodded, his eyes narrowing. 'Is Alice here—what of my son?'

'Your wife and son are both here and well. Alice has been out, but I saw her come in a moment ago from the window. Shall I ask her to come to you?'

'Alice hates sickrooms,' he said. 'I think she saw too much of them when she was a child. Her mother was very sickly for some years before she died and an aunt was similarly afflicted. Alice cannot bear the sight of blood or the stench of vomit.'

'I dare say no one likes it much,' Babette replied. 'But I am sure she would wish to see you now that you have come to your senses.'

'Are you?' John frowned. 'I am not so certain. We were much in love when we first met—but I think, perhaps, she has tired of me. She constantly asks when I am going to take her to court.'

'Well, you may do so now that you are both in Oxford. You have nowhere else to go, John, for both the castle and Brevington are lost to you. I rescued Alice's jewels and some gold, which she demanded from me, when I left Colby House.'

'You gave the gold to Alice?' John sighed. 'A pity. She will spend every piece on clothes or trinkets. It was one of the reasons I left her at the castle and did not bring her here—she cannot resist shops and pretty things. I indulged her when I could, but we had little until Father's estate became mine—and shall have even less now.'

Babette frowned. 'I am sorry, John. She asked for what was yours and I could not refuse her—after all, had you not recovered, whatever is left of your estate would have been hers in trust for your son.'

'And she could not wait to spend it.' John eased his shoulders. 'I do not blame you, Sister—and I thank you for coming. You could not have wanted to leave since you are to wed Captain Colby.'

'You know?' Babette was uncertain as she met his gaze, but she could see that something had changed. 'You do not mind?'

'Yes, I mind. I should prefer that you marry a Royalist, and a lord would hardly be good enough for you, Babs—but I know your heart is set on Colby. Drew says his cousin is a decent, honest man and I understand him to be wealthy enough to give you the life you deserve. I cannot even offer you a home, though your dowry should be safe. The Earl had charge of it, though I had applied for custody, but his Majesty had not yet released it into my hands. I think there is a quantity of jewels Mother left for you and perhaps the sum of five hundred pounds in gold, placed with the Jews of London, I believe. Not a huge amount, but more than I have left to me—and it will all come to you when you marry.'

'Has it all gone?' Babette looked anxiously at him. 'Can you save nothing? The land at Brevington is as sweet as ever, John. It is only the house that has been lost.'

'I might raise a loan against my revenues there to build a house, but for a start it would be modest—not what Alice would wish or expect.'

'You say I have five hundred pounds in my dowry. I would give you half…'

'Nay, Sister,' John said. 'It is generous of you, but I shall not take your money.'

'As James's wife I shall want for nothing. I am certain he would agree to share it with you.'

'No, I shall not take what is yours. If I have lost what I had—far more than you inherited—it is my fault and I must find a way to recover.'

'I am glad that you no longer forbid me to marry James. He wanted to ask for your permission, but we thought you would refuse to see him.'

'I might have done so before all this happened—but he took you both in and gave you shelter. Had I died Alice and my son would have had a home with you for a time. I am grateful and the least I can do is to give you my blessing.'

Babette felt tears sting her eyes. 'I am happier for it, John. I shall go down and tell Alice the good news.'

'If she thinks it good news...' John looked gloomy. 'Had I died, she would have been free to wed again—perhaps someone more worthy than me.'

Babette shook her head, but could not reassure him. What she had witnessed from her window had disturbed her, for Alice had been flirting with the Cavalier, even though she believed her husband lay close to death.

Leaving the sickroom, she went down the stairs to the parlour. The door was ajar and she could hear voices from inside.

'She forced me to go to that hateful man's house,' Alice was complaining. 'Now she comes here to nurse my husband and I am supposed to feel grateful—and if she saves him, what am I to do? I do not love him and I cannot bear…'

Babette felt the anger rise inside her. Without pausing for thought, she pushed open the door and went in, causing Alice to look startled.

'Your husband is better,' she said. 'Should you not hasten to his bedside and speak with him?'

Alice opened her mouth and closed it, a look of fury in her eyes. For a moment she could not speak, but when she did a stream of vicious words poured forth.

'And how have you managed that, witch?' she accused. 'He was dying. Everyone said he would not live the week—and now you tell me he is better. What witchcraft have you used to achieve such a miracle?'

'If I had used witchcraft, which I have not and could not, for I know none—you should be grateful to me. John is your husband and he loves you. You should be happy for his life.'

'Damn you! You shall not tell me what to do.' Alice rushed at her and slapped her face. 'You are a witch and you shall pay for what you just said to me.'

Pushing past Babette, she ran up the stairs. Instead of going into John's room, she rushed into her own and slammed the door.

Captain Richards had the grace to look awkward. 'Forgive me, I should leave...'

'My brother is recovering and will live,' Babette said. 'If you were hoping Alice would soon be a widow, you are mistaken. My brother would not be pleased to know that while he lay close to death you and she... Fear not, I shall not tell him, but another might.'

Captain Richards looked green. 'No, no, you misjudge me, mistress. I merely played the part of a good friend, hoping to cheer her—I am to marry an heiress of some fortune in a few months. Please do not attribute feelings or intentions to me that were not of my making.'

Babette's mouth twisted with scorn as he left the parlour hurriedly. He had merely been flirting with Alice, using her and perhaps hoping to seduce her—if he had not already. Alice would be a fool to desert her loving husband for such a rogue.

Babette sighed and stretched, feeling exhausted. She needed to rest after so many days of looking after her brother. His marriage problems were not hers and in the morning she would ask for her horse and return to Colby House with Jonas as her escort—and Maigret, unless she wished to remain in Lady Harvey's employ.

Tears stung her eyes as she went up to her little attic room and lay down fully clothed. She could not wait to return to Colby and prayed that James would have read her letter by now and understood. The sooner she was back with him, the better.

James had reached Oxford and looked about him, slightly ill at ease as he rode through the streets. There was no doubting this was a Royalist stronghold and if he were recognised he could be accused of coming here as a spy. The gates had been opened to allow traders and visitors to the city to enter and leave. He had been stopped by a guard and asked the reason for his visit.

'I am here on a matter of personal business,'

he said. 'I have come to fetch my fiancée and to buy a wedding gift for her.'

'Who is your lady, sir?'

'Mistress Babette is the sister of Lord John Harvey.'

'A true friend of his Majesty—pass, friend.'

James had wondered at how easy it was to enter the city. The questions asked had hardly been probing and only a few people were being checked and asked for papers or searched. Either the Royalists were very confident of their power here or someone was not doing his duty.

Without Babette's letter to assist him, James had no idea of where to find her. Oxford was a large place and it would not be easy, for he could hardly search house to house. He would have to ask if anyone knew where Lord Harvey was staying—and he had to hope that Babette had managed to help her brother, for if not there was no telling whether she was still here.

Babette asked John if he had any money to spare for her and he gave her ten silver shillings, apologising for not giving her more.

'It is enough for my needs,' she said. 'I hope to leave tomorrow and I shall need some food for the journey. I thought I would go to the market and purchase cheese, bread and honey. Plain fare will suffice until I reach Colby, but I must have enough to feed Jonas and Maigret if she wishes to return with me.'

'I would give you all I have, but I shall need something if I am to begin the work at Brevington. I must leave Alice here in Oxford until I can construct at least the shell of a house where she can live.'

Babette thought that her sister-in-law would much prefer to stay in Oxford, but made no comment. John must either make his wife obey him or face the consequences.

He had offered to escort her to Colby himself, if she would wait until he was strong enough, but Babette explained that she was in a hurry to return, and he accepted her decision.

'I cannot forbid you,' he said. 'You are of an age to make your own future—and I wish you well.'

Seeing that he was comfortable, Babette left the house and walked through the streets towards the market square. She must spend her few shillings wisely, because it would take her a few days to reach Colby and she might need some pence on the journey.

She had been walking for some minutes before she began to notice the odd stares some folk were giving her. Seeing a group of three women staring at her as she crossed the street, she caught a snatch of what they were saying.

'She's a witch…I heard it from Mistress Jones…'

Babette's blood ran cold. So the whispers had started here. She knew where they had come from, of course. Alice had accused her of witchcraft to her face and no doubt Mistress Jones had believed her—as she had believed all the other spiteful lies Alice had told her.

It was as well that she was to leave soon. She thought that it might not be safe for her to stay here long if terrible rumours had begun to circulate.

Now that she had reached the market, Babette began to make her purchases. She bought a large cheese, some apples, a pot of honey and a loaf of bread. They might purchase more bread on the journey, but she could not afford to buy better food and knew that she would need to give most of the food to her servants. Her purchases made, she turned to leave and then realised that a small group had gathered and were staring at her, blocking her path.

'That's the witch…'

'We don't want her sort here…'

'She should be stoned out of the town…'

'Put her in the stocks first and we'll show her what we do with her kind…'

Babette felt the trickle of fear as they advanced on her. How could she resist? There were too many of them—and yet she could not let them just take her. Looking about her, she decided that she would try to run to her left, but even as she started to edge away they were rushing upon her. She screamed as a stout washerwoman laid rough hands on her, pulling her to the far side of the square where the stocks for punishment were set up. Another woman grabbed a handful of her hair and a third wrested her basket with the food and her purse from her grasp.

Babette screamed again, but they had reached the stocks. She knew that they would lock her head and hands in place by means of a wooden yoke and then would throw rotten food at her. After she had been shamed enough she would be cast out of the city—unless they decided to hang her. Tears burned behind her eyes—it was so unkind to be treated thus and all because a jealous woman had named her a witch. Was she not even to have a trial?

'Unhand her, you wretch…' a strong voice cried. 'This woman is no witch, but a good, generous lady who gives her skill to help others.'

'James!' Tears trickled down Babette's cheeks as she saw him. For a moment she thought the women would defy him, but he took a pistol from his pocket, pointing it at the chest of the buxom harpy who had started it all. 'Oh, James!' Her chest was tight with emotion and she felt weak in her relief.

'Lay another finger on her—any of you— and I'll make you sorry you were born.'

The women looked sullen and muttered threats, but fell away, withdrawing to a safe distance to watch as James took hold of Babette's left arm, steering her away from the market. He propelled her along the street until they reached a quiet courtyard where a pleasant inn stood, then he allowed her to rest on a wooden bench.

'James,' Babette said as she sank down to the rustic seat, 'I do not know what I should have done had you not come—how did you come here to Oxford?'

'I rode in through the gates,' he said, his expression hard as he looked down at her. 'Why did you come here—and why were they call-ing you a witch? What have you done?'

Babette was conscious of the soreness where his fingers had dug into her arm. He seemed so angry and for a moment she did not know how to answer him.

'You had my letter?'

'There was no letter. Mrs Brisket told you left one, but it had gone—I thought that per-haps you had left me?'

'No, James,' she said, noticing the pulse flicking at his right temple. 'You know that I would never do so. I had no choice but to come since your cousin told me that John was likely to die if I did not go to him—and I think he would had I not nursed him.'

His expression did not lighten and his cold-ness hurt her. Why was he staring at her in such a way? 'He is better now?'

'Yes, though still too weak to get up much. He will recover, for all he needs is good food and his landlady will provide that for him.' She met his angry gaze. 'I was about to return. I came shopping for food for the journey—and then those women set on me...'

'Why should they call you a witch?'

'Alice named me so in her spite and the

word must have spread.' Babette tossed her head defiantly. 'It is my uncle all over again. All I did was to make my brother well again— but because Alice would have preferred to be a widow, she vented her spite on me. Mistress Jones must have heard her and gossiped of it. Alice complained of me to her from the start and she believed her.'

'She is an ungrateful, spiteful woman,' James said. 'I intended to ask your brother for his blessing—but we shall leave at once. You owe him nothing.'

'John has been understanding. He gave me ten shillings for my journey and he has so little—not even the money to build his house again—but he has given me his blessing.'

James's eyes narrowed. 'He has accepted our marriage?'

'Yes, for he knows my mind is set. And though he does not exactly like the idea, he will not forbid me. He says he can offer me nothing but his blessing...though in time the King may be applied to for my dowry, which is with the Jews of London.'

'And which his Majesty would take great pleasure in withholding because I am his enemy,' James replied, frowning. 'I do not care for your dowry, Babette. If you have inherited jewels belonging to your mother, I will try to get them when the war is over, but I can promise nothing.'

'I do not care for them if you do not,' she said and smiled at him, offering her hand. 'I have trinkets to remind me of her that she gave me before she died. All I want is to live in peace with you at your home.'

'Nay, Babette.' James's brow relaxed and he smiled slightly. 'You shame me by your goodness. Forgive me, I should have comforted you rather than frown on you, but I was angry when I saw what they did to you. I wondered what had caused their spite, but I should have remembered the way ignorant people mistake skill for witchery.'

'It seems that if someone hates you they will use the label of witch against you.'

'Alice is an ungrateful wretch to hurt you so.'

'It hardly matters since you came in time to help me.'

'Had I not done so…' He shuddered, his eyes dark with anguish. She saw it and smiled, holding out her hand to comfort him.

'Do not let them distress you, James.'

'The sooner we are away from here, the better!'

'I have the horses we brought from Colby,' she said. 'They are stabled at the hostelry—and Jonas and Maigret would wish to return with us, I think.'

'Then we shall go back to your brother's lodging house and ask them—and I shall speak with your brother. I would have things settled between us if I can.'

'Yes.' Babette held his hand tightly, her fingers entwining with his. 'If you do not mind, I would like to say goodbye to John. Alice does not behave as she ought to him and I fear for their marriage.'

James nodded. 'She is a selfish woman and such women often make their husbands' lives unbearable. I shall offer to make your brother a loan to help him rebuild Brevington. If he will accept my help, there is no reason why we should not be friends in the future—when this war is ended.'

'I wish it were ended now,' Babette said. 'But I fear the hatred is strong here and I do not think the King would make peace—he believes that he is the one who has been wronged by the men who speak and fight against him.' She looked at him anxiously. 'Should you be here, James? Are you not taking a risk?'

'I had to come, Babette,' he said, and his eyes were serious. 'I was afraid that you might suffer at your sister-in-law's hands—and it seems I was right. I dared not leave it to fate whether you returned or not—and I thank God I was in time.'

'Yes...' Babette shivered as she thought what might have happened had he not arrived in the market square at the right moment. She would not tell him that she had been forced to sleep in the attics or of the way Alice had taken every chance to spite and humiliate her. It no longer mattered. All that she cared for now was that James and her brother should make their own peace—and perhaps one day become friends.

John had risen from his bed and was downstairs in the parlour when they returned to the house. Looking at his face, Babette saw the terrible despair and asked what troubled him.

'It is Alice,' he said. 'We quarrelled earlier and she left in anger. I think she has gone to Captain Richards. She told me she wished I had died and that "that witch your sister had not cured you"—she hates us both, it seems.'

'Oh, John, I am so sorry,' Babette said. She

hesitated, then, 'If she thinks Captain Richards will wed her, I fear she is wrong. He will ruin her and desert her.'

'By God, I'll kill him if he does.'

'Would you take her back if she returned?' James asked, looking at him hard. 'If I should go after him and force him to release her…'

'I appreciate the offer, for I am in no case to chase after an errant wife,' John said and then sighed. 'No, I do not want her forced. If she comes back to me…we'll see.' He shook his head. 'Enough of my troubles. We must speak in private of Babs—and then I must arrange a safe passage out of Oxford for you both. Drew is due here at any time. He will see you clear, as he has more authority than I.'

'Yes, I know he was the fugitive some of my colleagues searched for when I stayed with Sir Matthew. I am aware that he is a clever spy and bears a price on his head, but I would not dwell on these things. He is my cousin and once my best friend. We are at war and must manage each for ourselves as best we can.' He turned to Babette. 'Go up and pack your things. We shall leave within the hour. To stay longer might endanger us both after what happened in the market.'

'What happened?' John asked, but Babette shook her head.

'It does not matter,' she replied and walked away, turning at the door as she heard a child's cry. 'What is that—she did not leave the babe?'

'Aye, she told me she wanted none of the troublesome brat. I must find a nurse for him somehow.'

Babette's gaze met James's, and he inclined his head. 'If you wish, we can give the boy a home with us until the war is over and you come for him.'

The look of relief in her brother's face made her smile. John would not have asked, but to know that his child was safe would ease the burden of grief for him. He could not have left the child with a nurse and been at ease, for children died so easily if neglected.

Running upstairs, she found Maigret nursing the babe. The maidservant was relieved to see her. 'The babe is sore, mistress. *She* would not let me use the salve you gave me to ease his bottom.'

'Alice has gone to visit someone so you may use the salve now,' Babette said, not wishing to betray her brother's wife. 'We are to take him home with us until John comes for him.

Pack his things and yours, for we must leave within the hour.'

'Praise be to God,' Maigret said. 'I have been praying that you would go home, mistress—and take me with you.'

'Go with God, both of you,' John said and leaned in to kiss Babette's cheek. 'Drew will see you through the gates and accompany you far enough to see you safe and then return. You have my blessing, Sister—and I shall come for the child when I have a home to take him to and a nurse to care for him.'

'I am so sorry, John,' she said. 'I know you loved Alice.'

'I shall always love her, but time heals in its own way.'

Babette nodded and walked to her horse. James tossed her up to the saddle and gave her the reins, gazing up at her earnestly.

'You are ready?'

'Very ready and eager,' she said, not trying to hide the way she felt. 'I shall be glad to be home.'

'And I,' he said. 'We shall have but a few days now, but we must make the most of them, Babs.'

'Yes, we shall,' she replied and then as he turned away to mount his own horse, she glanced at Drew Melbourne. 'I thank you for the safe passage you have secured for us, sir.'

'I gave you my word that I would see you safely home—and I do not forget that I owe my life to you. I am happy to repay the debt.'

'You will say farewell to Mistress Beth for me, please. We met but briefly, but I liked her. I hope that one day you will bring your wife to us as a friend, sir.'

'If ever we are fortunate enough to marry, I shall certainly do so,' he said with a rueful smile. 'My lady liked you, too, mistress—but her father will not part with her just yet, I fear.'

'I am sorry for you both,' Babette said, for she knew how it felt to wait for the end of the conflict and not to know if you would ever see the one you loved again. At least Beth and Drew were able to meet when they were both in Oxford, but Drew must be often on some secret mission for the King. She knew now that when he'd been injured both he and John had infiltrated a garrison of rebels and, when unmasked, had barely escaped with their lives. Had they been discovered in Sir Matthew's woods they would have been hung without a trial—and she might have been severely punished for helping them. She had not known the risk she ran and had James not been the man he was, she might easily have been caught when on a visit to the fugitives.

She had been fortunate that it was he and not some other Roundhead officer who had discovered her foraging in the woods. She drew close with him as they began to thread their way through the busy streets, smiling at him.

'I love you, James Colby,' she said. 'I cannot wait to be your wife.'

'I love you, my sweet lady,' he replied. 'Once I would have called you a witch in jest, but no more. Had I not come in search of you, I know not what might have happened here.'

'My brother would have saved me if he knew…but it might have been too late,' she replied and looked deep into his eyes. 'Only you would have walked into a Royalist stronghold in search of me, James. Did you not think of the danger to yourself?'

'I came alone, for I would not risk my men or my servants,' he said, his gaze warming her through to the heart. 'I thought your sister-in-law might have taken your letter, and I feared she meant you some harm. I had to come, otherwise I might have lost you.'

'I do not know why she should hate me, but I think she does.'

'Jealousy, perhaps?' James arched his brows. 'You are all that she is not and never could be.'

Babette arched her brows at him, but he merely smiled.

'I shall tell you when we are alone…when we are wed…'

Babette felt her cheeks grow warm and looked away, because the promise in his eyes made her tremble and burn with what she knew, but would not for her modesty name, as sweet desire. A tide of love, need and hot passion rose up in her. How much she loved this man, loved his strength, his gentleness and his honour. Hot betraying colour washed into her cheeks, and she lowered her eyes for fear that he should see her need and know how much she longed to be in his arms and feel his kiss.

Chapter Thirteen

James had arranged to meet his men at a safe distance from Oxford. When they reached the prearranged meeting place the men were waiting in the secluded clearing within vast woods. Drew said farewell and withdrew with the two men-at-arms he had brought with him to escort them clear of the city.

James thanked him for his good offices. 'I pray that we shall never meet as enemies on the field of battle, Cousin,' he said as they clasped hands.

'And I pray for a lasting settlement that will bring the country together again.'

James inclined his head, though he knew that Drew desired a different outcome to that dearest to his own heart. Drew would have his Majesty back on his throne, whilst James wanted a free Parliament elected by the people for the people. Their beliefs directly opposed and were unlikely to meet unless a sensible agreement could be found.

For a while after Drew had gone they rode in silence; then, glancing at James, Babette asked, 'It must pain you to know that your cousin is an avowed enemy to your cause?'

'It would if I dwelled upon it,' he agreed and smiled at her. 'I could never hate Drew, especially after what he did for us today—and yet I believe that all he stands for is wrong. If King Charles would but accept he is mere mortal man and rules for the good of the people and not by divine right, perhaps a truce could be called—a settlement whereby he was not an absolute monarch, a dictator, but a servant of the people.'

'Do you think Charles Stuart would ever agree to such restrictions?'

'No, I do not,' he said ruefully. 'His belief is so absolute that I think he would rather accept death.'

They were silent then for a moment, then James said, 'But we shall not think or talk of the war, Babs. We shall be wed as soon as we get home so that we can have a few days together. I had hoped for longer but it took me five days to find you.'

'I wish that I had not been obliged to leave your house, James.'

'I do not blame you, my love,' he said and sighed. 'Only this wretched war that obliges me to leave you. Had you ignored your brother's need, we should not have made our peace with him, but it has curtailed the time I hoped to have with you.'

Babette inclined her head. Theirs had been a love dogged by duty and regret on both sides, but now at last they were free to follow their hearts.

She felt a warm glow as he rode ahead to catch up with his men. He was a strong, handsome man and she loved him. Perhaps she would never be first in his heart, for he still loved Jane—but he cared for her. He had entered Oxford, knowing that he could be arrested and tried as a spy, for which the punishment was a terrible death—and he had saved her from a vicious mob.

She might not be his first love, but she would make herself so useful to him that she would be his last.

* * *

Mrs Brisket came out to the courtyard as they dismounted, looking anxious. She smiled a welcome as James helped Babette to dismount and came to kiss her on the cheek.

'I am so pleased to see you home, Mistress Babette,' she said, 'and you, sir.' Then, after some hesitation, 'There are visitors, mistress. They claimed to be your relatives and so I allowed them to stay, but I was not sure if I did right.'

Babette was mystified. 'I have only two relatives besides my brother and nephew—and that is Aunt Minnie and—' Before she could finish someone came out of the house and rushed towards her, crying her name. 'Cousin Angelina,' she said. 'How came you here—is my aunt with you?'

'She was afraid to come after the way you were turned from our house,' Angelina said and caught her hands. 'But I was sure you would take us in, Babs. Please, please do not send us away, for we have nowhere to go.'

'Nowhere to go?' Babette stared at her in surprise. 'How did you know I was here? And why have you nowhere to go?'

'We did not know. We came to ask sanctuary of my father's cousin and your housekeeper told us he was to marry you, but that you had been called to Oxford. She allowed us to wait for your return.' Tears were trembling on Angelina's lashes. 'My father is dead. They came one night at dusk just as we sat down to supper—twenty or more—and they accused him of being a traitor to the King. They said he would be tried and hanged for his crimes and arrested him but...he would not go with them and they killed him in the struggle.'

'Sir Matthew is dead?' Babette made the sign of the cross over her heart. 'I am so sorry. I bore him no ill will for what he said to me, for I know he was a superstitious man. I am sorry for your loss.'

Angelina shook her head. 'I do not care. He was so cruel to Mother and to me after you left, forbidding us any pleasures. I think he had lost his reason.'

'Oh, Angelina. I am so very sorry, my dear. But why did you say you had nowhere to go?'

'The Royalists gave us an hour to pack our personal things and then they made us leave with what we had on a small cart. After we had gone they set fire to the house.'

'Set fire… Oh, no, how could they?' Babette said. 'That was surely not necessary.'

'They said it was a nest of vipers and that my father harboured spies and traitors. We could not think of anyone else who would take us in, for we knew that the castle had fallen—and as we passed Brevington we saw it had also been burned, though some of it still stands.'

'John is to build a new, smaller house there soon,' Babette told her. 'As far as I am concerned you may stay here—at least until somewhere of your own can be found…' She glanced at James and he frowned slightly, then replied that she might do as she wished since she was the mistress of her own home.

He had turned away to talk to his housekeeper and then to his steward. Angelina tucked her arm through Babette's and they went into the house together. As they entered the larger parlour at the front of the house, Aunt Minnie came towards them, looking anxious.

'I am sorry if we are a trouble to you, Babette,' she said. 'Had I anywhere else to go…'

'Do not be foolish, Aunt. I know well that it was not your choice to send me away. My uncle was a superstitious man and took a dislike to me—but I have the lace you gave me, which was my mother's, and I shall use it for my first child's christening gown.'

Her eyes were suspiciously moist as she looked at Babette. 'It is generous of you to speak so fair to me, Babette. I always knew that neither you nor your mother was a witch— and it was a lie that she ill wished that man. What happened was that he tried to touch you in a way not befitting an older man with a very young girl. Your mother was so very angry. She told him that she would see him punished—that he would be placed in the stocks for other men and women to throw rotten fruit at and then given fifty lashes.'

'My uncle thought she cursed him.'

'No more than any mother who saw a man try to interfere with her young daughter—but they were friends and when he lied and told your uncle that she was a witch and had cursed him, he believed her. When you wanted to stay with us he reminded me of it and told me that if he saw a sign of witchcraft you would have to go. I was so sorry that he should think your brave action, which saved Captain Colby from bleeding to death, was a sign that you had used the dark arts. Had I argued with him he would have said I was bewitched and must be whipped to drive the demons from my body.'

'He did beat you, Mother,' Angelina said, 'because you said that you were sad Babette had left us. And when I refused to believe ill of my cousin, he locked me in my room with bread and water until I apologised to him.'

'I am so sorry that what I did caused so much trouble for you both,' Babette said. 'Please forgive me.'

'It is I who begs forgiveness,' her aunt said. 'I have missed you, Babette—and if you will permit me, I should like to see you wed.'

'I shall be happy for you to attend me at my wedding, Angie,' Babette said. 'And it is good to have you here, dear Aunt. Please, let us forget what happened, for it can only cause distress to remember.'

'I shall never allow anyone to call you names again,' Aunt Minnie said. 'I was afraid of Matthew, but in future I shall speak out what is in my heart.'

Babette thanked her and then went upstairs to see how Maigret and Baby Jonny had fared on the journey.

'Do you mind that my aunt and her daughter came here?' Babette said later that evening when they were alone. 'I could not refuse them a home here—until such time as they can find a cottage of their own.'

'Sir Matthew was my cousin, even if I did not always like his principles,' James said and reached out to touch her cheek. 'You are always generous, my sweet Babs, and it is one of the reasons I adore you. Of course they must have a home here, but I shall find them a house in the village where they may live as they please, and give my cousin's widow an allowance. It is the least I can do for her. Perhaps we may find a husband for Angelina soon enough. In time, I may be able to recover some of their property, for the land he farmed is rightly theirs.'

'Angelina used to like Cavaliers for their gaiety and their clothes, but after what happened I think she may have taken a dislike for them. I think had I been there I should have found such men to be my enemies.'

'In times of war these things happen. At least your aunt and cousin were allowed to take some of their belongings and leave. My cousin brought his fate on himself, for he should have been more discreet in his dealings with others. I dare say he upset his neighbours and was reported to the Royalist troop. I do not excuse them, but in war...' He shook his head, looking grave.

James left the rest unsaid and Babette understood. He, too, might be forced to do things he found unpalatable in war, but it did not mean he would relish the task.

'I would not have my cousin pushed into a marriage she could not like. She must marry for love, as I know she would wish.'

'I am all for that,' James said and reached out to touch her cheek. 'I loved Jane so very much and I was devastated when she died. For a long time I thought I should never love again, but then you came into my life—a bold, beautiful woman who stood up to me fearlessly and sneaked out to tend a Royalist spy. I should not have fallen in love with you, Babs. I should have ridden away and forgot you, for your beliefs were so opposed to mine—but I could not. That indefinable thing we call love bound me to you in a way I never was to Jane. She was my friend and sister—and you are the woman I adore with my heart, my mind and my body. I think in a way Herbert was right—his sister was not meant for marriage.'

As he gazed into her eyes, Babette trembled. Could he really mean what he said? Was it possible that she had come to mean so much to him?

'Do you truly love me, James?' she asked, her breath catching in her throat. 'I thought… that I could never be first with you…that you would always love her.'

'As I do, as the sister she was to me. Had we married it would have been a terrible mistake, as I believe Jane knew. She loved me and everyone took it for granted that we should marry, so when I asked her she could not refuse me, but she begged for time. I should have known that what I felt was not the love a man feels for a woman he wishes to lie with in the marriage bed. And if I did not then I know it now, for I have found a woman who can match me in all things, a woman who hungers as I hunger. A woman who is strong enough to share all the things of life, both pleasure and pain. Yes, I desire, but I know also that you are the better part of me…so much more than I deserve.'

Babette's cheeks were warm as he laughed softly in his throat, pulling her close into his body. His breath was warm on her cheeks and she felt herself tremble as he bent his head, touching his lips to hers. A ribbon of fire shot through her, making her breathe more heavily and moan as she arched into his body, melting in the heat of his passion.

'I love you so very much,' she said and her lashes were wet with the tears that slipped silently down her cheeks. 'You must promise me to come back to me as soon as you can.'

'As soon as I can,' he promised against her lips. 'But for now I want to think of tomorrow and tomorrow night when you will be my wife in truth and I can take you to my bed.'

'We have so little time,' she murmured huskily. 'Why wait until tomorrow night when you can have me now?'

'I have waited so long, my darling,' he said. 'I can wait a little longer, for I shall not dishonour the woman I love above my life.' His lips brushed over her skin, his tongue lapping at the hollow in her throat. She longed for him to take her down to the soft rug of sheepskin that lay on the floor, but she knew that her honourable rebel would not step over the line he had set himself. 'Tomorrow will be all the sweeter for waiting another day.'

A gurgle of laughter rose in her throat as she pressed herself closer. The night between might seem an age, but then she would find

her happiness in the arms of a man she had
once thought her enemy.

James's neighbours and friends had all accepted the invitation to his wedding, and the
church was filled to capacity to see them take
their vows. As yet the hand of the Puritans
had not touched their place of worship, and
the sunlight struck on the huge silver cross and
candlesticks that graced the altar as they knelt
to take their vows.

Babette was dressed in the gown she had
begun before she left for Oxford, which Mrs
Brisket had finished for her.

'I did it in the hope of your return, mistress,'
she had told Babette when they spoke in private. 'I hope that I did as I ought?'

'It was a wonderful surprise, for I had nothing suitable to marry in and should not have
cared to wear an old gown for my wedding.'

She had a dress of pale grey silk trimmed
with silver lace, a veil of old Spanish lace,
which had belonged to James's mother, and a
coronet of silver wire set with semi-precious
stones. Angelina told her she was beautiful
and hugged her until Aunt Minnie told her to
be careful of Babette's gown. Angelina wore

a dress of pale blue, which colour she had always loved to wear until her father forbade her to wear anything but black.

'I am so happy to see you wed Cousin James,' she said. 'I longed to come and stay when you were at your brother's castle, but I am even happier here.'

'We shall see each other often, even when you move into your own house. James must leave in a few days and you will be my companion and stop me moping while he is gone.'

'I shall visit every day if you will have me.'

Babette said she would be very happy to see her. James had found a house not dissimilar to the one they had lost in the village for them; it would take Angelina only twenty-five minutes or so to walk to the manor every day to visit, which she would find easy, unless the snow was deep on the ground.

Angelina acted as Babette's attendant, and Aunt Minnie gave her away. The vicar was pleased to see that she had relatives to attend her and more than delighted that her brother had given his consent to the wedding. Babette would have liked John to be present, but she knew he was in Oxford and still recovering from his illness. When the war was over she believed he would visit them, but until then perhaps it was best that he did not. James's people were staunchly for Parliament and it would not do to stretch their loyalty too far.

When they returned to the house, it was to discover that Mrs Brisket and her minions had outdone themselves. The wedding breakfast was a collation of pies, roasted meats, capon, baked carp and pigeon in wine. There were side dishes of sweetbreads, stewed raspberries and custards, also plums preserved in wine and delicious creams laced with brandy. A dish of apple tarts was placed in the centre of the table and proved irresistible for all the younger people—and the wine had been sweetened with honey to make it pleasant on the palate.

Babette could not stop smiling as she greeted her guests and made them welcome. Everyone spoke of feeling pleased that James had found someone he could love, several mentioning his sweet, lost Jane. However, Babette no longer felt that prick of jealousy, for she knew she was loved and would always be first with him.

When at last their guests had gone and Aunt Minnie had taken Angelina off to their new home, Babette stood within the circle of her husband's arms, her body thrilling to the heat of his and the throbbing evidence of his desire.

'Shall you go up and prepare for bed, my love? I shall not be long.'

Babette kissed him and left his arms reluctantly. Alone with Maigret in the chamber she would from now on share with her husband, she stood to allow her maid to disrobe her and then sat on a stool to have her hair brushed so that it fell in shining folds to the middle of her back.

'You have such pretty hair, mistress.'

'Thank you.' Babette felt ridiculously shy as James knocked at the door and then entered, Maigret leaving by way of the dressing chamber so that they were completely alone.

James came to her, gazing down into her face for such a long time that Babette was anxious, thinking that something must have displeased him, but when she tentatively asked if anything were wrong, he shook his head. His hand reached out to caress her cheek and he smiled.

'I was thinking how lovely you are in every way and how fortunate I am to have found you, my darling.'

'Oh, James…' Sighing, Babette moved into the circle of his arms and, giving herself up to his kiss, she felt her bones melt with pleasure. Suddenly, she was on fire with need and desire and pressed herself against him so that she could feel his hardness through the thin material of her night chemise. 'I love you so much, my beloved. Make me yours, James. Show me what it is to be a woman in the arms of the man who loves her.'

'I shall always love you,' he murmured throatily as he gathered her up and carried her to their bed. 'Even when we are both growing old and past the heat of youth I shall want you to lie beside me, my dearest love.'

He was gentle as he lay her down and then stripped away his robe, coming to her naked as she watched, a faint colour burning her cheeks as she saw and understood what she had only sensed previously. His manhood was proud and vital, as was the rest of his strong body, making her tremble with delicious anticipation.

'We have no need of this between us,' James said and lifted her to tug her night chemise over her head. It resisted and she helped him to remove it, their efforts to be rid of the offending garment making them laugh and easing any tension that Babette might have felt. She lay looking at him trustingly as his eyes moved over her. 'You are more beautiful than I could ever have imagined.'

Bending his head, he began to kiss her. First her lips, then her eyelids and her nose. Kisses trailed down her white throat to the little pulse spot at the base and then down to her breasts. With the tip of his tongue he circled her nipples, which had peaked with thrusting need under his attention. A moan left her lips as she felt the stirring of something wonderful deep inside her. Oh, what was this lovely melting feeling that made her feel boneless, weightless, as if she floated on air? His lips and tongue travelled over her navel, made her squirm and cry out with need, though she hardly knew what more she needed. His hand parted her legs, and he kissed the insides of her thighs, the slight roughness of his tongue making her cry out in pleasure. When he buried his face in the curls that covered her most feminine place, inhaling her scent, she moaned and arched beneath him, her body calling for a fulfilment she had never known or realised she wanted.

When at last he entered her, she felt a sharp

brief pain that made her still and caused him to look at her.

'I have hurt you, but it is always so and will not happen again.'

Babette raised her love-drugged eyes to his and whispered through lips swollen with his kisses, 'Please, continue. The pain was slight and I want you inside me. I am yours, make me yours in truth, James, take me with you where you go.'

James resumed his rhythmic motions, his manhood filling her, stretching her, making her melt with pleasure as the world seemed to move beneath her and she lost herself, becoming a part of the man and he a part of her. When at last she felt his climax and hers followed seconds after, she was spun away, feeling as if she were foam on a gentle sea that expended itself against a golden beach. She was warmed as if by the sun, boneless, complete and satiated, no thought but of his body clasped next to hers as they lay entwined, neither wishing to break the spell that held them.

Later, they talked of their joy in each other, of their hopes for the future. James wanted a son and two daughters, if God should grant them such good fortune. Babette laughed and said that as long as she had him and children she would not care what sex they were. James talked of his plans for the estate and the house, for the land he would buy to make their children more secure.

'The house is yours to refurbish as you will,' he told her as he lay stroking her hair, letting the silken strands run through his fingers. 'I have made a will naming you as the guardian of our children until they reach the age of nineteen. The house is yours and an income, and the children will receive their portion when they reach the age of nineteen or marry...'

'Hush, my love,' she said and pressed her lips to his. 'I know that you have done everything that needs to be done to protect us—but let us not speak of the need. God send, you will live to be ninety and I a few years less so that we are not parted for too many years before we meet again in paradise.'

James laughed as he gazed down at her, raising himself on one arm. 'Think you we shall be allowed through the pearly gates or mayhap 'tis the other place...?'

'Oh, no,' Babette said and smiled lovingly into his eyes. 'You will live a long and exem-

plary life, as I shall—and when the appointed
time comes we shall be together.'

'I would burn in hell if it meant being with
you,' he said throatily and began to caress and
kiss her once more. 'But you are an angel and
it is more likely that you would have to come
there in search of me.'

Babette knew that he was teasing her, making her laugh so that she would forget the pos-
sibility of his being killed in battle. He'd told
her that he expected Cromwell to force a decisive battle before the year was out and he
must be with his commander. Being the man
he was, he had settled with his lawyers that
she and any child she bore him would be provided for, but there was so little time and none
to spare for worrying.

They spent the night in making love, sleeping and waking, roused to loving again and
again, until James said no more lest she was
sore and she begged him to kiss her again.
So then he loved her, bringing her to a glorious climax once more, but did not take his
own pleasure, saying that he knew she would
suffer. Babette slept again, having known the
most exquisite pleasure of her life.

* * *

In the morning James was up early. When she woke she heard voices in the courtyard and, rising, went to the window to look out. She saw her husband and his men training, working hard at their swordplay and fighting as if for real, which they must again in a few days.

Her throat caught, but then James called enough, and she watched as he went to the pump and stuck his head under the cold water, letting it cascade over his body. Remembering how she had watched him from a window in her uncle's house and felt immodest for having seen him without his shirt, she smiled. She knew every inch of his body now and it was glorious.

They had two more days together before James must leave, and she would make the most of them. Chores could wait; she would have time enough for sewing and making lists when he had gone.

Dressing quickly, she went down to the courtyard just as James was about to enter the house. He saw her and came towards her immediately, a look of love in his eyes.

'Did we wake you, dear heart?'

'No. I should normally have been up long before this,' she said. 'What must you do today, James?'

'Nothing. We have done our training for the day—the rest of it belongs to you. What would you have me do?'

'Could we take food to the river and sit in the sun? I would have a day of rest and pleasure, James. I want to spend every minute I can with you until you must leave.'

'Then I shall oblige, my lady,' he said and reached out to draw her in close, gazing down at her with passion. 'We shall take a blanket and find a secluded spot. I know just the place.'

James's secluded spot was idyllic, the riverbank fronded with willows that sheltered them from prying eyes if any had been there to see—but James had left instructions that the river was off limits for the day. Since his word was law, because his people loved and respected him, Babette knew that no one would come near. They were completely alone to do whatever they wished.

Babette removed her gown and went into the river to paddle in the shallows because the day was hot. James stripped off all his things, came in with her and then pulled her down into the water so that her shift was soaked through. Then he pulled it over her head so that they could both frolic naked in the cool water. Babette screamed and laughed as he tried to show her how to swim. She kept one foot on the ground, but at last he encouraged her to trust him and she managed to keep afloat for a few strokes before going under.

'You'll learn in time,' he teased and kissed her. 'I'll make a bather of you yet, my love.'

Babette laughed and splashed him, but two could play at that and she came off worst, screaming as she ran on to the dry bank and flopped down on the blanket. James followed her from the water and she saw that his need for her had manifested itself. He wrapped her in his shirt to dry her and then lay down beside her on the blanket, drawing her into his arms.

They made love swiftly, passion flaring, and afterwards lay in each other's arms until James declared he needed food and they dressed and ate, feeding each other with the good pies, tarts, cheese and bread their housekeeper had provided.

Afterwards, they talked, sang a little and recited poetry to each other. It was late in the afternoon when they wended their way home again. One of their precious days had gone, but it would provide memories to ease their loneliness when the time of parting came.

Three nights and two days were the length of their time together and how swiftly the time went. On the morning that James left, Babette rose as soon as he did and went down to the parlour, making sure that he ate a proper breakfast.

James looked at her gravely across the table, where the remains of their repast lay scattered. She saw that he was ready to go, his mind on other things, though he reached out to touch her hand.

'You know that I have no choice. I would never leave you, my darling—but my duty calls.'

'I know you must go. I have my duty here, which will keep me busy for there is much to do. I have John's child and my aunt and cousin to keep me company. I am fortunate, James—and these past few days have been the happiest of my life.'

He rose, and she rose, too, moving into his arms. Bending his head, he kissed her on the lips with a sweetness and tenderness that brought a lump to her throat.

'Do not come out to the courtyard. I must be strong for my men. They, too, leave loved ones and friends. They, too, answer the call of duty and know not if they will return. Let us say goodbye here, Babette. I shall write to you when I can give you an address to reply, but that may not be for a while.'

Babette let him go with a smile. She went up to her chamber and began to tidy it, resisting the urge to look out until she heard the order to move off. Then she ran to the window and saw James look up briefly. She held up her hand in salute and then he had turned away and was riding at the head of his men.

She stayed at the window and watched until the column of fighting men had disappeared from view. It was then that the wave of loneliness seemed to swamp her, but just as she felt she would die of her despair, her door opened and Maigret came in, carrying her nephew.

'He is teething again, mistress,' she said. 'The poor little fellow is in such pain. Have you something to ease him?'

Babette blinked hard and put away her tears. She was the mistress of her husband's home and his people would rely on her to keep them healthy. Her brother's son needed her and so did everyone else who lived at the manor. She lifted her head, pride flowing into her and strength—strength to do what she must until her love returned.

Afterword

$\sim\!\!\infty\!\!\sim$

It was a glorious summer day, very similar to the one that they had spent by the river during the war—the day that she believed her first son had been conceived. Babette looked at her family gathered on the lawn. Her two sons were playing ball; Jamie, the elder, being very gentle with his brother, younger by just eighteen months. Their sister, Barbara, was just four months old and had been conceived when James returned from the war.

It had been a long war and Babette had spent many lonely months without her beloved husband, but he had visited her whenever he was able and their second son, Tomas had been born when he was home on leave with a troubling wound towards the end of the conflict. Babette had given birth easily, which had not been the case when Jamie was born, but Mrs Brisket had seen her through it and she'd recovered by the time her beloved husband returned once more.

James saw her looking about her and came towards her, glancing at the babe in her cradle. 'Is anything wrong, dearest?'

'No,' she replied, smiling at him. 'I was just thinking how lucky we are.' She glanced across at her brother, who was talking to his son, the eldest of the children present. 'I wish that John could be as happy and settled as we are.'

'He has at last ceased to grieve for Alice,' James said and frowned. 'He grieved sorely when he learned she had died of a fever, but I think he has begun to feel better now. Perhaps he would not wish me to say—but I think he has met someone, a rather pretty girl who seems to be fond of him. Her name is Gillian and he might marry her in time. I believe he is in a way to being happy again.'

'Yes, perhaps,' Babette said. 'The letter that came this morning—was it from your cousin Drew? I know he went to France when things turned out badly for the King.'

'Yes, it was from Drew. He remains in

France and from what I hear is still not married to his Beth.'

'He should have done as my brother did. John made his peace with Parliament and was allowed to keep Brevington, though the castle has gone for ever.'

'He seems not to care, and Gillian is a simple country girl. I think she will be happy in the house John has built for himself and his son. It is a sturdy house and we shall visit him there next month.'

'He has achieved a great deal with your help,' Babette said and looked at him with love in her eyes. 'We have so much. I feel so fortunate…'

'We are very fortunate,' James said and reached out to drop a kiss on her forehead.

He had been offered a post in London as a reward for his good service, but unlike Cromwell had decided that he would not accept. He wanted neither a pension nor honours, but a simple life at home with his wife and children. In London, Cromwell was beset by arguing factions and near driven mad by their demands; it was not the life for James.

Watching his sons, he smiled. He had said he wanted one son and two daughters, but in truth he cared not one whit. As long as his wife and children thrived, he was content.

'You are beautiful and I could tarry with you all day,' he said softly. 'Tonight I shall show you how fortunate I think myself—but for the moment I should look after our guests.'

Babette nodded, watching as he moved away to talk to their neighbours and friends, and enquire if they had all they needed. She felt a wave of happiness engulf her. The lonely years were past and she could look forward to a long and glorious life with her beloved husband and their children.

* * * * *

HISTORICAL

IGNITE YOUR IMAGINATION, STEP INTO THE PAST...

My wish list for next month's titles...

In stores from 4th April 2014:

- ❏ Unlacing Lady Thea – Louise Allen
- ❏ The Wedding Ring Quest – Carla Kelly
- ❏ London's Most Wanted Rake – Bronwyn Scott
- ❏ Scandal at Greystone Manor – Mary Nichols
- ❏ Rescued from Ruin – Georgie Lee
- ❏ Welcome to Wyoming – Kate Bridges

Available at WHSmith, Tesco, Asda, Eason, Amazon and Apple

Just can't wait?

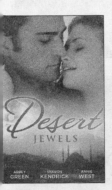

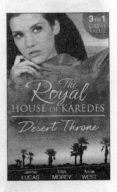

The Regency Ballroom Collection

 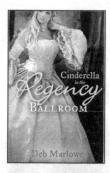 

A twelve-book collection led by Louise Allen
and written by the top authors and rising
stars of historical romance!

Classic tales of scandal and seduction in
the Regency ballroom

**Take your place on the ballroom floor now, at:
www.millsandboon.co.uk**

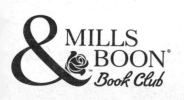

Discover more romance at

www.millsandboon.co.uk

- ❤ WIN great prizes in our exclusive competitions
- ❤ BUY new titles before they hit the shops
- ❤ BROWSE new books and REVIEW your favourites
- ❤ SAVE on new books with the Mills & Boon® Bookclub™
- ❤ DISCOVER new authors

PLUS, to chat about your favourite reads, get the latest news and find special offers:

- Find us on facebook.com/millsandboon
- Follow us on twitter.com/millsandboonuk
- ❤ Sign up to our newsletter at millsandboon.co.uk

M&B_WEB